T0194236

The Mind of
a Heart

The Mind of
a Heart

Anne Dennish

To order additional copies of this book, contact:
Xlibris
844-714-8691
www.Xlibris.com
Orders@Xlibris.com
838649

In memory of Eugene Snyder, my college professor, who believed in this book from the moment that I wrote it.

For Donna and GT

With love and gratitude to God and the Universe for getting me here.
And I love where I am.
Namaste

Prologue

John and I had been corresponding by email and telephone on a daily basis for several months now. Our earlier conversations consisted of catching up on each other's lives, our families and what we'd been doing for the last twenty five years. We also spoke about how much we had missed each other throughout the years. Soon, we began a string of emails that we called our "Confessionals." They were the heart and soul of "us," consisting of why we broke up so many years ago, why it didn't work out and more importantly, why neither of us ran back to one another. Our confessionals were intense and sometimes emotional, yet proved to be quite therapeutic for both of us. We'd both wondered for all those years where we went wrong and why we never got back together...

Until now.

We both agreed that neither of us had ever stopped loving the other and in fact, had never loved anyone else in the way that we had loved each other. Our love was born out of youthful innocence so many years ago and, although time had taken us in different directions, the love we felt for one another had never lessened. We had simply tucked it deep inside of our hearts. Perhaps we were waiting until our paths crossed again to see if those feelings still existed.

And they did.

John was a poet and wrote the most beautiful emails to me, ones filled with love and romance, all the things I wanted and needed to hear. This went on for just about a month when I received an email like no other…

My dear sweet Jersey girl,

I hope this email finds you happy and well. I'm leaving on a business trip next week and will be in Kennett Square. I'll be there for three days and I want you to do what it takes to meet me there. We've been writing and calling each other for months now and it's about time we get together in person. I know it won't be easy for you to get away, but I need you to do this for me. I need you to do this for us.

I love you so much, my girl, and I need to see you, kiss you, hold you. I need more than a voice on the phone or words on a computer screen, babe. I need you.

I want to run my fingers through your hair, kiss your neck and caress your body. I want to make love to you with abandon.

Meet me in Kennett Square, babe. I want you more than words can say… John

And this is how it all began

Chapter 1

I read John's email over and over again, all the while fantasizing about what it would be like to make love to him again, yet at the same time wondering how I'd ever get away for three days. I'd never gone away by myself before and never left my children for more than an hour or two at a time. How in the hell was I going to pull it off now? How was I going to break a pattern of always being home to one of going away, and of going miles away?

I sat back in my chair, closed my eyes, and imagined what those three days would be like and what they would *feel* like.

My heart was racing, my mind wandering to places it hadn't been in years. My thoughts were crossing a line in my head and I wondered how I would cross that line with my body. I envisioned our bodies twisted together, naked in a pool of sweat from intense lovemaking. I had loved this man once with a passion that most have never experienced, a love so dangerous that once you gave into it you would never be able to get out.

I could feel myself filling with a rush of excitement at the thought of being with John again and I could feel my body beginning to respond to the thought of his touch. Slowly, my head rolled back, my eyes closed, and my back began to arch. It was as if this fantasy was becoming reality and a body that hadn't felt like this in decades, was now making up for lost time.

The thought of being locked away with him in a hotel room was beyond my wildest imagination. It was a place that I thought I'd never dare to go, a place I had never even dreamt of going to, yet here I sat not thinking of whether or not to go, but instead of how I'd get there.

I had to go, I knew that, yet more importantly, I wanted to go. I'd move heaven and earth to be with him. Now, the task of finding a reason for going began. I opened my eyes, drifted back down to reality, and hit the reply key on my computer:

"My love, I'll be there. Nothing could keep me away. Until then, I'm yours forever… Me"

We had met in the seventh grade. He had dark hair and sometimes wore glasses, giving him a nerdy look, yet he had a smile that lit him up from the inside out. He sat behind me in social studies class and had an uncanny knack for making me laugh - really belly laugh! He'd sing me songs before class started. "Pinball Wizard" was his favorite and soon became mine. He was this innocent, shy boy, most likely not even thinking close to what I was.

I hated social studies yet he made me look forward to it everyday. Just knowing he was there, sitting behind me, made my day. I could feel his feet on the back of my chair and every once in a while he'd give it a shove, giggling as he saw my body jerk forward. He didn't know at the time that I would smile every time he did that.

I remember our eighth grade class trip to Washington, DC. I'm sure it was Colleen that made John and I sit together on the bus. John was extremely giddy, covering his nervousness, I'm sure. All I wanted was for him to hold my hand. I even strategically placed my hand near his so he could do just that. Yet the most I got from him was a light touch, on which he commented how soft my hand was.

"Boys!" I thought to myself, feeling annoyed and ignored. "What's wrong with them?"

Seventh and eighth grade would come to an end, with no hand holding and no kiss, but unbeknownst to John and I, the foundation of something that he and I would have never imagined was now set in place.

Chapter 2

The day to travel to Kennett Square was fast approaching and I had conjured up a story of it being an "early birthday" gift for myself. The hotel was only about fifteen minutes from Colleen's house, which added a perfect reason for going there. I had told Richie that it'd be nice "me" time along with being able to spend time with my oldest and dearest friend. Surprisingly, he was more than supportive and thought it was a great idea. He always despised how much time I spent in the house and with the kids all these years, so I guess it was a relief for him to see me step out of my comfort zone. Then again, I think he despised the fact that my time was spent on our kids rather than focused on him, yet at this moment I could have cared less what he thought. I was just thankful that he was letting me go at all.

I booked myself into John's hotel and had all the plans set in place and ready to go. Colleen and I actually would spend some time together, seeing that John really was going to be on a business trip. Richie was going to take some time off from work to watch the kids, so all that was left for me to do was to pack and to find the courage to go through with my plans.

John had already filled me in on what to expect when I saw him. He hadn't changed much since high school, except for the fact that his dark brown hair was now peppered with gray!

"Haven't we all gone a little gray?" I mused back. "I thank God everyday for my hairdresser, Mark. He has the magic touch when it comes to my hair!"

"I'm in really good shape, great shape, actually. Been working out all these years and some people have told me I look like a model," he said, sounding a bit full of himself, but I guess when you kill yourself trying to look like a model you have every right to flaunt it, except that now I was wondering what he'd think about me after all these years.

The last time John saw me naked was when I was 18 years old. At that age I had a flat belly and a tight butt! Now, after almost 25 years, I definitely showed signs of having had children. My belly was definitely not as flat as it used to be, and as for my butt? Well, let's just say that "tight" was no longer an exact description. As for above the waist, well, nursing and weight loss can wreak havoc on your breasts. What in God's name was he going to think of me, I wondered as I peered into the full length mirror of our bedroom. Oh, well, there's not much to be done about it now. This is as good as it gets, at least until after this rendezvous!

"It'll definitely be a light's out night, for sure," I thought. "Candlelight should hide all these imperfections quite nicely. At least I hope it does." I added "bring A LOT of candles" to my already growing list of things to pack. As time would go on, I'd realize that I should have packed my sanity and morals with me as well.

Everything happens for a reason and this adventure must have a reason. I just hope it's what my heart already knows and wants.

I went to my favorite lingerie shop the next day. I started going there once I lost all the baby weight from the last pregnancy. I browsed through the store, wondering what John would like to see me in. I had asked him by email a few days ago and in true "guy" fashion, he said "I'd like to see you in nothing!" Hmph, not the answer I wanted to hear and although it sounded romantic, to a woman rekindling a love affair after 25 years it sounded more frightening to know that he'll be looking at me that closely. Well, "nothing" may be well and good for him, but I'd like to be in something sexy and beautiful, two words I haven't felt like in many years. Besides, he can see me in nothing after he's stripped me slowly of something, yet when he does, he'll be stripping off more than lingerie from me. He'll be stripping off my values, morals, and the trust so many, including my husband, have in me.

"Okay, it's time to shake this feeling of guilt," I'm telling myself in my head. It's time to get this shopping done and go home.

And so I did, deciding on a black lace bra and matching panties, black being the most deceivingly thinning color and one which I knew I looked good in.

I was getting nervous as the days passed and soon found myself on the day before the trip. I was leaving tomorrow to see John after all these years. I had gotten my haircut and colored, shaved all the necessary body parts and waxed my eyebrows. I treated myself to a manicure and pedicure and made sure that my skin was as soft as it could be for him.

I packed my clothes, taking my time to pick out just the right things, hoping all the while that I wouldn't be in them for too long when I saw him. I wasn't counting on too big of a sexual night on our first night together, neither of us had ever crossed this kind of line before, so I didn't want to get my hopes up.

Truth be told, I would be fine with just hand holding and kissing all night long, yet I did want him, more than I had ever imagined that I would.

Neither of us had ever had an affair before and I didn't know exactly what to expect. Suppose he got there with such a case of guilt that he wouldn't be able to go through with it? Suppose he takes one look at me and isn't completely turned on? My mind was racing with thoughts of the unknown - and I was scared - scared he wouldn't want me.

The sound of the kids downstairs brought me out of my daze and back into the real world of marriage and motherhood. I zipped my suitcase shut and brought it downstairs.

I loaded the car and went about my normal routine of wife and mother, all the while knowing that this time tomorrow I was about to add another role to myself: that of John's lover and that of an adultress.

I remember the first night we made love. We were barely eighteen years old and had been dating for only a few months, yet we were madly in love with one another. The night was planned for John's house. I wore baby blue corduroys and a white shirt, not paying too much attention to what was on underneath. After all, my mom still did my laundry and at this age I had no valid excuse for sexy lingerie. It would have been a dead giveaway to her as to my loss of virginity!

I was so nervous and shaky as I prepared myself for the evening. I heard my parents talking to someone downstairs and it took only moments before I realized that the other voice I heard was Johns'. I began to sweat and couldn't wait to see him. I spritzed myself with the perfume that he had bought me and proceeded slowly down the stairs.

There he was, tight blue jeans and an Inlet-Outlet surf shop t-shirt, and of course, his white sneakers (my idea of sexy!) He couldn't have looked sexier if he tried. My heart began to race. His long dark hair was neatly combed as usual and he smelled great! He looked up at me as I hit the bottom step and smiled at me, his eyes shining.

"Hey, babe, ready for the movies?" he asked, both of us knowing that this was our cover-up story for the night.

"I sure am!" I answered back, smiling at him, knowing what we had planned.

My parents told us to have a good time and in true parental fashion added the infamous "and don't be late!" I really do believe that that line must be written in a parent handbook somewhere.

John grabbed my hand, kissed me and led me out the front door. We walked out to his black Chevy Chevelle, which he sweetly named "Rosie." He opened the car door for me and settled me into my seat. He looked at me and leaned over to give me a long, wet kiss, his tongue melting onto mine. He patted the bench seat next to him, his usual signal for me to slide over next to him. I did just that and he slid his arm around my shoulders. I never felt so safe.

There was an ice cold six pack of Bud on the floor and I opened one for each of us. The beer was a welcome sight knowing how nervous I felt. We took a few sips and John pulled out of the driveway. We were on our way to his house to make love for the very first time and I was sure it wouldn't be the last.

He turned on some music, a "Lynyrd Skynyrd" eight track that we loved, and started singing to me, just as he did in seventh grade. Even at this young, innocent age, I knew that this was what heaven must feel like, because I was definitely floating in the clouds.

John kissed me at all the red lights and squeezed my shoulder now and again with his hand. The car windows were open, our hair blowing wildly in the wind, music surrounding us in the car. We pulled into his driveway just as his mother was pulling out. We parked and went over to her car to talk for a few minutes.

"I forgot my wallet," John yelled over to her. Wow, what a quick thinker he is!

"Johnny, you should be more careful! I'll be home really late so don't wait up for me," she said as she gave us a quick wave and drove down the driveway.

We smiled at each other, knowing that the whole night, or most of it, would be ours and ours alone. We walked hand in hand to the front door, stopping briefly on the porch. Johnny pulled me into his arms, kissing me hard, his hands running down my back, stopping to grab my bottom for a squeeze. "I love doing that," he would always say.

Then he stared deep into my eyes, so deeply that I do believe he was staring right into my soul.

"Ready, babe?" he asked with a smile that only he could deliver.

"Yeah, I'm ready," I answered back.

We went into the house and headed straight to his bedroom. I loved his bedroom.

Everything in it depicted the exact person he is. He had Led Zeppelin and Peter Frampton posters all over his walls, his guitar standing in the corner. A lava lamp was on the dresser right along with a strobe light. The room smelled like his cologne mixed in with weed. It was his smell and I loved it.

John handed me another beer, which I drank down quickly. He took the can from my hands, set it down on the floor, and kissed me.

This was the first time for both of us. Two eighteen year old virgins ready to lose it all to each other, to give each other something that we'd never given to anyone else. We were about to join our bodies together as one, and as I thought of how we'd be soul connected from this moment on, I became excited in a way that I never had before.

John turned off the lights, lit some candles and put on some music, not loudly like the other times we hung out in his room, but quietly.

"My romantic boy," I thought to myself.

He walked over to me and I was suddenly feeling really nervous. I could feel my body reacting to what was about to happen and felt as though I was trembling. I wasn't sure what I was supposed to do, and I'm sure he could sense that, so he took the lead and took my hand.

He undressed himself first, leaving only his briefs on. When I looked down I could see what it was that I was soon to have inside of me. It both terrified and excited me all at the same time! He slipped off my shirt and fumbled with the button on my pants. We giggled just a bit but that was short lived as he managed to unbutton them and slide them off of me. He danced my body over to his bed and gently laid me down onto it. He stood at the side of the bed looking deep into my eyes while he slipped off his briefs and tossed them on the floor. He leaned down to take off my bra and panties.

"My God, you are so incredibly beautiful," he whispered as he slid down to kiss me. At that moment I felt like my mind had drifted into a place that it had never been before and I never wanted to lose this feeling. I wanted my mind to stay in this place forever. He kissed me on the lips while caressing my breasts with his hand. He soon found them with his mouth, kissing and sucking on my nipples ever so softly. Within a few minutes he spread my legs apart with his hands, caressed me for a moment or two, and then gently, oh so gently, entered me, our bodies becoming one.

It felt so good to have him inside of me and within seconds we were making love in perfect rhythm with one another. He thrust deeper and deeper inside of me, sounds coming from each of us that I swear was the sound of our souls. He kept moving and moving inside of me, first slowly, until he movements became harder and faster. I could tell by his breathing that he was about to come inside of me, and I knew from how wet we both were that I was going to come with him as he did. Suddenly, it was that one thrust that he let go that filled me inside with all of him.

"My God, I just made love to the boy I love with all my heart, my soulmate," I thought as my breathing began to slow back to a normal rhythm. And with that, he slid down next to me, kissed my forehead that was now covered in beads of sweat and took me into his arms.

"I love you, babe, I love you so much, and someday soon we'll make it all forever. You and I together forever and always, the way it should be,"

he promised. My heart was filled with so much love at that moment, yet at the same time, I was scared to death at how intensely dangerous this love between us really was.

And twenty five years later, it was becoming more and more apparent just how dangerous that love really is.

Chapter 3

The chatter of the kids downstairs pulled me out of my sleep. As I struggled to wake myself up I suddenly realized what today was - it was THE DAY! More importantly, I knew that tonight would be THE NIGHT! I kicked off my comforter and slid out of bed. I grabbed my bathrobe, threw it on, and went into the bathroom to brush my teeth, then I walked slowly down the steps to find the kids watching television, the older ones grumbling about having to watch the younger ones "little kid" show. My mind quickly slid into "mommy mode" and I began my task of making their breakfast and tidying up the house, knowing that in just a few hours I'd be in my car and on the road to Kennett Square. I was too nervous to eat, so once the kids were all settled at the table eating their pancakes, I ran upstairs to dress and head out for coffee and a cigarette, both of which I was desperately in need of at the moment.

John monopolized my thoughts on the entire drive to my favorite coffee house. My mind kept wandering to thoughts of what the night would bring for us. I had a slight fear that tonight would make or break us, yet the real fear was of having an affair and how it may change who I am. Truth is, it already has changed me and even though we haven't connected through the physical aspect yet, we were both certainly deep in the throes of an affair.

What would happen to me if this "affair" wasn't enough of him as time went on? How would this change my already doomed marriage or my ability to be the mom I am and want to be? Oh my God, here comes the doubt.

And here comes the guilt.

I wanted a perfect life with my husband and children, and it wasn't this "affair" that was hurting my marriage, it was Richie and I who hurt each other through many years of moving in different directions and away from each other. It was his illness that took a toll on him and on the rest of us. I didn't want to try anymore. I was there as a mom and nothing else.

Yet, here I find myself wanting to be perfect for John, perfect in every way that a person can be. No pressure here, though, I thought. I grabbed my coffee, had a cigarette, and headed back home to a home that would never be the same again after tonight.

When I walked back into the house, I stood and looked around for a moment. Life seemed just as it always was. Everything was in place and the kids were going about their usual routine of bickering and playing. Richie was parked in his usual spot in the living room, perched in the chair by the window. He was sitting there with his laptop, checking his emails and whatever other sites he kept a secret to me. He spent all his time in that chair, so much so that the impression of his "arse" was clearly imprinted into the cushion. This is my life, or was.

John's emails and stolen phone calls deep into the night had changed my life. Only God knew how my life was about to change after he and I got together tonight. Yet still, I was willing to take the chance, to risk the life I was in, if only to see if the love was still there, and if the emotions of that dangerous, once in a lifetime kind of love, were still on fire.

I stood for what seemed an eternity, looking at this picture of a happy family who wasn't happy at all. It was as if I was looking at a mirage. Yet I wasn't.

I went upstairs to shower, taking more than my usual five minutes to do my hair and make-up. I needed to look perfect today. I needed to BE perfect tonight. This was quite a lot to ask of a woman who's been in this house for the last fifteen years tending to her husband and three children.

I looked through my closet with more care than usual, picking out a pair of tight, low rise jeans and a white v-neck Gap t-shirt. I opted for white Keds sneakers seeing that the weather hadn't warmed up enough yet for my sandals.

"Not too fancy, but it gets the point across," I thought out loud. A spritz of "Heavenly" perfume and I was ready to hit the road. I walked downstairs wondering if anyone noticed the apparent bounce in my step. I grabbed a red hoodie from my son, the one he always thought I looked very "cool" in, and I wondered if "cool" mattered to John.

Richie was still sitting in the chair as I walked into the room. I announced to him that I was ready to leave.

"Hey, you look really good! A real hip chick," he commented as he looked up briefly from his computer. "Have a great time with Colleen and enjoy yourself. The kids and I will be fine. You deserve this time for yourself. It's about time you pulled yourself out of here and this stupid rut you've been in for so long." He just had to say "stupid," didn't he, I thought. Richie was famous for screwing up a complement but I didn't care anymore. It makes it easier for me to leave and go see John without any guilt, just contempt.

"Thanks, I think," I mumbled back to him.

I searched the house to round up my three babies, giving them each a kiss and a hug and the standard "mommy line" of "Be good!" They were busy doing their own thing and barely looked up as I said good-bye. Billy and Jonah seemed to pull away from me a bit as I said good -bye, most likely because I was interrupting the video game that they were deep in thought playing.

I stepped back and took one last look around, knowing that when I came home from a weekend away that it would all look different to me, that it would all feel different. Nothing stays the same and this was a journey that was so foreign to me...yet so familiar.

I went back up to Richie to say goodbye and give him last minute instructions for the kids. He never got up to kiss me goodbye, only simply looking up to shoot me a quick smile. Just as well, I thought. I needed to leave now. My gut was beginning to feel strange, a feeling I'd never felt before. Was it guilt? Was it sadness? I wasn't sure, but I knew one thing to be true: if I didn't leave now, I may never leave at all.

"Just go already," he insisted, interrupting my train of thought. "You're wasting time, so just get on the road and don't worry about us. We'll be fine. Call me when you get there so I know you're safe."

Safe. What in the hell was safe at this point? "Get out now, or you'll never go," I kept telling myself inside my head. "Just go."

"Okay, I will. See you all in a couple days," and with that, I was out the door. I got into my big old Suburban. Sexy? I think NOT! I placed my coffee cup in the holder, threw in my Lynyrd Skynyrd CD, the one that John and I shared a deep love for, and drove out of the driveway. The butterflies in my stomach were unbearable and I wondered, if in fact, they didn't feel more like bats! I had no idea what lay ahead of me tonight, but I did know I was ready. Ready for change, ready for love, ready to feel something, feel anything, again.

And I'd been ready for twenty five years.

It was a cold Valentine's Day morning when my phone rang. It was John. He was calling to see if I wanted to go to the mall with him tonight and at 17 years old, who didn't want to go to the mall?

"Hey, want to hit the mall tonight?" he asked, making it sound as though he were asking me out on a date rather than a friendly jaunt out to the mall.

"Sure, do you want me to meet you there or do you want to pick me up?" I asked innocently. After all, I'd been dating someone for a few weeks and John and I had had nothing more than a friendly relationship at school.

"I'll pick you up, say around 6? Can you be ready?" he asked.

"Works for me, John, I'll see you tonight," I answered, wondering where this invite came from and what his intentions were.

Short and sweet, with not too much conversation, but my curiosity definitely peaked. He knew I had been going with Rob for a few weeks, so why was he asking me out now? Well, it could be that my instincts were wrong, and maybe it just was a friendly outing to the mall. Yet again, I don't believe that this was a random, innocent call. I knew better.

I ran downstairs to let my mother know my plans.

"Mom, I'm going to the mall tonight with John," I told her, knowing that if I asked to go, I would have left the window for discussion wide open for her to say "no."

"What about Rob? Doesn't John know you're seeing him?" she asked, sounding like a typical mother who sensed trouble looming ahead.

"Geez, Mom, it's just the mall. Besides, John and I are just friends. And yes, he knows all about me dating Rob, okay?" I said, hoping it sounded convincing. The expression on her face told a different story, yet happily, she didn't elaborate on what she was really thinking. She'd been down the dating road in her day and was definitely wise to the tricks of the trade, but my mom usually kept her mouth shut and let me learn things on my own.

"Well, just don't be too late. It's a school night. And what do I tell Rob if he calls?" she asked, trying to be the "cool" mom by getting our stories straight.

"Oh, tell him I'm out with Colleen," I answered, knowing that Rob would never find out seeing that he was miles away at college.

She shook her head in agreement and went back to her ironing, a mundane task that she loved, and why that is, I'll never know.

The afternoon flew by and after a quick dinner of steak and potatoes, I went up to my room to get ready for my "date" with John. A few minutes later he was pulling into the driveway. He got to the front door just as I was walking out of it.

"Hey, I was coming to the door to get you. It's the gentleman thing to do, 'ya know?" he laughed.

"Oh, shut up! Let's go, it's freezing out," I joked back, hurrying him out the door and to his car.

It had snowed a few days earlier and the air felt icy. The snow was still on the ground and piled up in huge mounds where the plows had pushed it. I was dressed in jeans, a bulky sweater and my heavy winter ski jacket, not to mention snow boots. But not John. He was wearing tight jeans, which outlined what a cute butt he had, a plaid flannel shirt, and a bright, red sleeveless down vest. I couldn't help but notice just how cute he looked. We got into his car, which he left running so that it would be warm when I got in.

"Got the car nice and warm just for you! Now, take off that big 'ol coat and throw it in the back!" he joked with a sarcastic, authoritative tone, yet I found myself liking this tone. This night was going to be interesting to say the least, I thought to myself.

"Warm? Warm you say? It's hotter than hell in here!' I joked back as I threw the coat in the back seat.

He laughed out loud as we got on the road to the mall.

We made small talk on the drive up, chatting mostly about school and the Winter Ball we had both attended with other people just the week before. This mindless chatter seemed to work because before we knew it, we were at the mall. John pulled into the parking lot and found a spot far away from the mall, right in front of a large mound of snow. There were no lights where we were parked, just the light of the moon bouncing off of the snow bank.

"Let's just hang out here," he said. "I really don't feel like doing the mall."

"Okay, that's fine," I answered as I began to wonder what he was thinking and what his plans were for tonight. Truth be told, I had an idea of what he had in mind and I was not about to complain. I had always liked this guy from as far back as seventh grade and he looked pretty damn cute tonight!

John reached over in front of me, brushing my knee as he did so, and pulled out a Meatloaf cassette which was in the glove box. My heart began racing at his touch. He popped it into the stereo and turned it up a bit.

"Did you ever hear of this group before?" he asked. "They're great - one of my favorites."

"Nope, never heard of 'em," I answered. I sat back and listened to the tape and soon realized that I was also listening to John sing along. He loved to sing and it brought back memories of him singing to me in our seventh grade math class.

"I'm beginning to like this band, too," I thought to myself. Then again, maybe I liked them so much because John did. No matter the reason, he was right about them being great.

He reached under his seat and I could see out of the corner of my eye that he had pulled out a small bag of weed. I kept staring at the snow bank as he rolled a joint and was getting nervous because I had never gotten high before. I didn't know what to do, so I just pretended that I wasn't paying attention to what he was doing.

"What, you've never gotten stoned before?" he said jokingly to me.

"No, never," I answered matter-of-factly.

"Well, you wanna try it? Now would be a good time for a first!" he joked back. "Trust me, it'll make you feel great - nice and mellow. Honestly, I wouldn't let anything hurt you. Promise," he said, and fool that I was, I believed him.

"I don't know," I said hesitantly, "I'm nervous. I don't want to go home stoned out of my mind."

"Stop worrying so much. It won't last all night and if it's your parents you're worried about, don't. They won't know a thing by the time I take you home," he pushed on. I was feeling a bit pressured but I knew I had to try it, if not for me, for him.

John lit the joint, took a few hits, and handed it to me. It was actually kind of nice, I thought, not much different than smoking a cigarette, which he and I both did, just a bit stronger. We passed the joint back and forth, watching to make sure the mall police didn't find us. John took a big hit, leaned over to me, and kissed me, blowing the smoke into my mouth. I held it in until the kiss broke and I exhaled. Our eyes locked and I was starting to feel the effects of the weed.

"Well, babe, how 'ya feeling?" he asked, a huge smile on his face. "Did you like that last hit?" And I knew he meant the kiss.

"I loved the last hit and I'm feeling really good, nice and mellow, just like you said," I answered, wondering if my words were slurring or not. John was right. I felt so mellow and calm and I'm sure that I was smiling ear to ear at him.

"I knew you'd like it and I knew you'd really like that last hit. Now, the trick is to smoke a cigarette right after you get high. It'll make you feel even higher!" he said.

Even higher? My God, I thought, where is this night going?

He lit a cigarette and shared it with me. I felt wonderful. I liked this getting high thing. My body felt all warm and fuzzy from head to toe.

I looked over at John and saw his glassy eyes staring at me, a wide smile on his face. Our eyes were suddenly locked together when he said...

"I love you."

He said it so matter of factly and with that he leaned over and started kissing me! This sure was a big change from the shy, seventh grade boy I remembered.

He put his hand on the back of my neck, under my long dark hair, and slowly pulled me towards him. As he did this he was moving my hair to one side and before I knew what was happening, he was kissing the side of my neck. I could feel my body responding as his soft kisses traced my neck, moving down to my shoulder. He pulled back a bit of my bulky sweater and kissed my shoulder before he moved up, where his mouth found mine. He was holding my face with both hands as he pressed his lips tightly to mine and within seconds his tongue found its way into my mouth, until it connected with my own tongue. We kissed like this for what seemed like forever until one hand slid down from my cheek to my shoulder, then to my waist where he slowly found his way up under my sweater. His hand ran up my bare skin until he reached my breast, which he began to caress gently. We were making out feverishly, groping each other all over. The high from the weed was getting stronger and stronger and the windows of the car were covered in the steam made from the heat of our bodies.

Before I knew it, Johnny had slid me down onto the seat, his body on top of mine, kissing me like I'd never been kissed before. I kept hearing the same Meatloaf songs playing over and over again which meant that we'd been at this for quite some time. I loved kissing this guy and I could tell in more ways than one that he felt the same. He came up for air and looked at his watch. It was almost eleven o'clock. My God, we'd been going at it for almost four hours! But, sad to say, it was time to get home. I was going to be late as it was and I'm sure that I'd have a helluva time getting up in the morning.

We sat up and I adjusted my sweater. We shared one more cigarette together, all the while smiling at each other like two little kids in a candy store! John's eyes were actually twinkling and that wasn't from being high. He was happy!

"I'd Do Anything For Love" started to play and John started to sing along:"and I would do anything for love, I'll never lie to you and that's a fact" and with that John touched my cheek ever so lightly and said "this song is for you. Always remember it, always remember tonight, and always remember me." And he was right, I will remember it all, forever and always.

I lost my senses and I couldn't tell if I was high from the weed or high from how I was feeling about him.

I think it was "him."

We left the mall, and despite my father's rules of "no sitting in the middle of the seat," I slid over next to him. Our bodies were molded into one another as if the Universe had made each of us specifically to fit one another. We remained that way the whole drive home. As we pulled into my driveway and parked, John played "my" song one more time.

He grabbed me one last time before I went into the house and pulled me close. His arms were wrapped tightly around me and mine around him.

"I love you," he said, kissing me all over my face, then grabbing my hand and kissing the top of it.

"I love you, too," I said back, planting one last kiss on his mouth.

I told him to stay in the car as I ran into the house. There was no need for him to get out and be cold, yet he insisted on walking me to the door, holding my hand until we got to the front door. He raised his hand to run his fingers through my hair, kissed me again, and with that he turned to leave.

I stood on the front porch and watched him walk to his car. He got in, threw me a last good-bye kiss, and drove off.

I ran into the house and headed straight for my bedroom. I sat down on the edge of my bed thinking about the last few hours I'd just spent with him.

And suddenly it dawned on me: I had just fallen in love with the man of my dreams, my soulmate.

What now?

Chapter 4

The drive to Kennett Square would only take about an hour and a half, which was a short amount of time, considering the amount of thinking I'd been doing lately. I often found myself thinking of this whole thing for hours and hours. I knew that the right thing to do was to turn around and go home to my husband. I was married, for better or worse, and this was it. Affairs are against the rules, both Gods' and mine, but I'd spent so many years doing the "right thing" and doing everything for everyone else that I felt it was time to do something for me. For the first time in forever I was happy, and not the happiness that comes from your children doing something spectacular, or your husband giving you a beautiful piece of jewelry - no, this was a happiness that lit me up from the inside out. It was a happiness that came from being loved by the man I've loved all my life. This was "my happiness" and no one else's and for the first time I felt as though this is what I deserved. I deserved to be happy and loved and I'd finally found it. I'd just found it in a way that I shouldn't have but I didn't care anymore. I'd spent too many years being unhappy and unfulfilled. It was my time now and I was willing to see this night through, no matter the outcome by morning. John was worth the risk and worth the effort to see if we really did still love one another.

Before I knew it I could see the sign for the hotel up ahead. Looks like all that thinking made the drive seem as though it was just minutes long. I turned into the parking lot, shut off the car, and pulled out my suitcase. I walked towards the front desk, where a heavy set, middle aged woman was waiting for me.

"Hi, there. Name?" she asked.

I gave her my name and signed the paperwork.

"So," she began, "are you here alone for a vacation or on business?"

Oh, no, I thought, she wants details! "No," but what I really felt like saying was, "I'm here to have an affair with my old high school sweetheart. We're both married to other people and wanted a nice hotel to commit adultery in."

But of course, what I thought wasn't what I said.

"Small mommy vacation for two nights, that's all," I answered.

"That's wonderful! Your husband must be a really wonderful guy," she said, but little did she know. I wanted to tell her that she could have him.

"I'll send up some goodies for you to relax even more. Enjoy your stay, honey."

"Thank you, that's sweet of you. I'm sure I'll enjoy whatever you send up," I said as I was trying to leave the desk and head to my room.

"How about some nice bubble bath for that Jacuzzi tub in your room? And if you'd like, I'll send up some wine for you. Just tell me what you like and I'll have our concierge run and get it for you," she said.

"Wow, what a nice idea! Bubble bath would be perfect, and as for wine? White Zinfandel," I answered, knowing that it wouldn't be just for me. I'd be sharing the bubbles and the wine with John.

"No problem. Now you go and get settled in, honey. I've kept you talking far too long for a mommy who's here to have some time alone," she said, as she picked up the phone to call the concierge.

"Thank you," I answered as I grabbed my key and headed to room 323.

I got into the elevator and pressed three. I could feel myself getting more and more nervous on the ride up. Oh my God, I thought, this is really happening. This isn't a dream or a fantasy. I'm about to cross a line that I never thought I would have. I was the girl who always thought badly of people who had affairs, yet never say never, I've learned, because here I am doing exactly what I judged others for.

And now I understood how they felt and how I ended up just like them.

I found my room and walked in. There was a Jacuzzi bathtub sunken into the floor next to my bed with a full view of the television (not that we'd be watching much of it!). There was a knock at the door and for a split second my heart jumped because John would be knocking at my door in another hour or two, yet I knew it was the woman from the desk. True to her word, she was at my door with a small bottle of bubble bath and a bottle of wine only minutes after I got here.

"Here you go, *mommy*," she said, as if to remind me that I was a mommy, not a woman or soon to be "adulteress."

"You throw these bubbles into your tub tonight and relax. Have a glass of wine or the whole bottle!" she laughed. "Don't think about your kids or your husband, just think about you! You'll be back home before you know it, so enjoy this time!" she said, and I swear I think she skipped out the door.

"Believe me, I won't be thinking of the kids or my husband while my lover and I are in the tub together doing God knows what!" I was thinking of saying, but of course, I didn't.

But she was right - I am a *MOMMY!*

And I was hoping that by the time John arrived I would in fact be able to turn myself into a *woman!*

Oh, God, I thought, what am I doing? Can a woman with children and a body that sure shows the effects of pregnancy on it pull off being attractive and alluring to a man who shows no signs of aging other than gray hair? What in God's name had I gotten myself into? I'll be crushed and what little self-esteem I have will be out the window if he takes one look at me and runs the other way, although John would be polite enough to say that he couldn't do this, take me to dinner, and call it a night.

And then he'd never call again.

Oh, hell, if it weren't for low self-esteem I'd have none at all. I wanted to be everything to him, everything he dreamed of, everything he wanted, and everything I was at eighteen.

Enough of this! I took a deep breath and two of my headache pills, which always managed to mellow me out, had a cigarette and decided to just take my chances. I'd put myself together the best I could and if that wasn't good enough for him, then dammit, he wasn't good enough for me!

The blanket of mellow from my pills descended upon me and I began to feel calm, really calm.

Okay then, I thought to myself, on with it.

I was lying in bed, hoping that I could get back to sleep after being abruptly awakened by my younger brother and sister bickering downstairs. They do this to me every morning. All they do is argue!

"SHUT UP!" I yelled from my bed, and with that my brother came running into my room spilling out his side of the story and my sister was just steps behind him telling me her side. It sucks being the oldest!

I sat up in bed and told them to calm down so I could listen to both their sides. Of course, that only brought yet another argument over who goes first, because whoever went first had a better chance at lying which in turn would only infuriate the other one more.

"You know what? I don't care what you're arguing about! Enough is enough! It's my prom night and I need to look good for John tonight!" I yelled back.

And then they stopped in their tracks. All you had to do was mention the name "John" and they would stop arguing. They adored him and would do anything to please him or get one of his big belly laughs out of him. He liked them, too, especially since he was the youngest of five.

"Fine," my brother grunted, "you watch your show first, but then it's my turn." He always gives in, I thought. My sister had the stubbornness of a mule and could hold her ground longer than anyone I knew. Even though she was younger than me I tried my hardest to never get into a fight with her because she could be brutal!

"See, if you had just done that in the beginning, none of this would have happened to you, MOMMA'S BOY!" she taunted my brother. She

always had to get the last word in and with that, she was out of the room and down the stairs to watch television.

"Sorry I woke you up," my brother sheepishly apologized. He was warm and compassionate and I could tell by his demeanor that he felt badly about waking me up. "What time is John coming over? Early?" he asked excitedly.

"It's okay, Bo," I said. "Bo" had been his nickname since he was a baby.

"I was half awake anyway. John won't be able to stay too long, we're meeting some friends at the Station House before the prom and we don't want to be late. Hey, if it makes you feel better, he's sleeping over so you'll be able to see him in the morning, okay?" I said, hoping this would satisfy him.

"Okay," he said, a bit disappointed yet excited knowing that John would spend time watching cartoons with him in the morning. I think he used my brother as an excuse to watch them anyway because I knew he'd never admit to me that at this age, he still watches cartoons!

Now that the kids' fight was settled I rolled out of bed and slowly made my way downstairs. I grabbed a cup of coffee, which I could tell by the taste had been sitting there for a while.

"Mom, any chance you could make a fresh pot? This stuff tastes awful," I asked, knowing that since it was prom day I could ask almost anything of her and she'd deliver!

"Sure, I'll make you some. Want some breakfast, too?" she asked, dropping the basket of laundry she was carrying onto the couch.

"No, I'm too nervous. Coffee is okay," I answered.

"Coffee and a cigarette, right?" she asked back with her usual sarcastic tone. She knew I smoked and hated that I did, even though she did it herself.

My usual response to that is "no response" so I went back upstairs. The smell of fresh coffee would waft its way up the stairs when it was finished brewing. Now began the task of getting myself ready for prom night!

I looked at my dress which was hanging on the back of my door. It was the true epitome of a "prom dress." She was peach colored with satin ribbons. I was sure that John would love her. He hadn't seen her yet. "I want to surprise you," I had told him after I bought it.

I could smell the coffee and within seconds my mother was yelling up to me that it was ready. I went downstairs and poured a cup, cream and three sugars, just like John, and took it upstairs. I sat down at my make-up table and proceeded to do all the primping that an eighteen year old girl does for prom night. I saved my nails for last.

The morning and afternoon passed quickly, thank God, because my stomach was filled with nervous butterflies! This would make for an interesting night once the drinking began. I'm sure by the time we get to the "Station House" my jitters would be alleviated, after all, I'd be with John and no one could ever make me feel so safe and relaxed as he could.

I had finished my hair and make-up and was sliding on my dress ever so carefully. Next was a cute little pair of panties that I had bought and managed to slip past my mother. I'd most likely throw them away after tonight just so she wouldn't know that her daughter had bought something so "sexy!" Then again, knowing John, he'd keep them tucked under the front seat of the car with his weed! Next was my pantyhose, then my strappy white sandals bought specifically to match my dress. One last look in the mirror and everything was in place.

I didn't know that John had already gotten here until I heard his voice from downstairs talking to my parents. I spritzed myself with perfume, grabbed my bag, and walked slowly down the stairs, knowing full well that he would be standing at the bottom. He looked up and smiled, yet this wasn't a look I had seen before. This was different.

"Oh, my God! You look so beautiful! My God, babe, look at you!" he said, as if stunned that I could look that way, yet in reality, I knew he wouldn't have thought that at all. His gaze was fixed on me, and I had to get down to the bottom step to force him out of this zone!

"Well, thank you, kind sir!" I joked back. "And look at you!"

I walked over to him where he grabbed my hands and gave me a kiss that was proper enough to give in front of my parents.

"Okay, let me get a good look at 'ya, then," I said jokingly, eyeballing him from head to toe.

John had decided on a dark burgundy tuxedo with dark satin trim to match. He looked quite handsome. He turned around slowly for me to see all of him. I checked him out and as I went from his head to his toes I started to laugh. On his feet were his brown leather school shoes! Now I really began to laugh!

"Okay, okay, so I forgot to rent the shoes! HA, HA, HA!" he said sarcastically, with just a slight sound of annoyance in his voice.

"It looks fine, babe, really. I love it. Now you won't look like all those other stiffs wearing plastic shoes. Not only that, your feet won't be hurting and we'll be able to dance the whole night away!" I said, kissing him on the cheek, running my fingers through his hair. He loved when I did that and had often said that I would be the only girl he'd ever let do that!

"Pictures!" my dad yelled as he directed us to the fireplace.

"Wait!" I yelled, "flowers!"

"I have flowers, too, babe, just for you!" John yelled, rushing out to the car to get them and rushing back in just as quickly.

He handed me a beautiful little nosegay of peach and burgundy flowers, "our colors." I, in turn, pinned a carnation tinted with burgundy onto his lapel. Our ensembles were now complete and so were we being together.

We stepped in front of the fireplace and my Dad began snapping pictures, posing us side by side, staring up at each, and him with his arms around me. You name the pose and he shot the picture! I think he must have taken about thirty pictures and I couldn't wait until they were developed later that week so I could see them.

Now that our "photo shoot" was done, it was time to head to the "Station House" to meet our friends. I grabbed my white shawl and John and I headed off to begin the night of our "Senior Prom!"

He opened the car door for me and I slid all the way over to the center of the seat, wanting to be near him in the worst way. We opted to take "Rosie" to the prom, unlike all our friends who were driving their parents' Cadillacs and Lincoln Continental's.

"Rosie" was our car and it just wouldn't have been the same to leave her out of such a special occasion. After all, she's been there in some of our most important moments!

John hopped into the driver's seat and we were off to the "Station House" Or so I thought.

Chapter 5

I called home to let Richie know that I had arrived safely at the hotel, but all I got was the answering machine. It's just as well, I thought. I began unpacking my clothes and when I was done I sat down in the comfy chair by the window that overlooked the courtyard. It was filled with beautiful flowers and bushes, large trees placed throughout with wooden benches underneath their shade. I was hoping that John and I would spend some time out there.

I sat in that chair, thinking to myself how quiet and peaceful it all was and that I WAS ALONE FOR THE FIRST TIME IN FIFTEEN YEARS!

And so far, I loved it!

I ordered up some coffee and fresh fruit to tie me over until John arrived. I had my coffee and a few cigarettes, then laid down on the bed. I fell asleep for about an hour - a sleep filled with the same dreams I have every night: dreams of John.

I woke up slowly, with that feeling of wondering "where am I?" I'm not used to being alone in a strange place, so it took a few minutes to come out of it. Once I shook the sleepiness from my body, I freshened up my make-up, fluffed up my hair a bit, and had another cup of coffee. John would be here shortly and I wanted to make a good first impression when he walked through the door.

I wondered if he would come in and grab me in a passionate kiss or walk in, give me a small kiss, and start up with some small talk. God,

I was beginning to sound like a teenager again, worrying about things I hadn't since then.

I looked down at my watch and realized that he'd be here any minute. I looked in the mirror one more time, checking my hair and make-up yet again. I decided to wear a pair of stonewashed jeans and a white t-shirt along with white sneakers. I could always change after I knew where the evening was going, then again, clothes may become optional as the night goes on!

I ran into the bathroom to brush my teeth and spritz on some perfume. Now I'm ready. I was more than ready for anything he had to offer.

And then there was a knock at the door…

I was so nervous as I went to answer it, yet felt more excitement than I had in years! I opened the door and there he stood in the gray business suit he had described to me in detail. His hair was shorter than I remembered and all gray!

It felt as though we were standing there for a lifetime, yet just as I was hoping he would, he handled it all. He walked through the door and closed it. We stood facing each other, gazing into each others' eyes. I could feel tears welling up in my eyes and I could see that he was tearing up as well.

"My God, babe, you're eighteen! You're the same sweet girl who stole my heart a lifetime ago and the girl who owns it now," he said, a tear running down his cheek. He was still the hopeless romantic that he had always been. For a brief moment I wondered if he acted the same with his wife, but I had to pull my thoughts back to this moment, to him and I, because the reality is that we belong to other people. Yet my heart was bursting with happiness knowing that I was exactly what he had hoped for me to be, and more importantly, I was who he wanted.

"John, I've had kids, believe me, I've changed!" I said back to him.

"Well, babe, you wouldn't know it to look at you. You're still as beautiful and sexy as I remembered, even more now! I still can't believe I'm looking at you," he excitedly said, as if he was dreaming, yet he wasn't. "Now, give me a turn, girl, I want to see the whole package!" he said with a dirty gleam in his eye.

Great, I thought, now he wants to check out my back end. Well, at least I'd been working out for a few months now so it shouldn't look too bad! I did exactly as he asked and I gave him a spin. When I turned back around to face him he was just standing there smiling at me.

"God, babe, look at you! Unbelievable!" and with that my boy took me into his arms and kissed me just as he did on that Valentine's night at the mall, the first time we kissed, and the moment that we fell in love with each other.

We kissed for a few minutes before we sat down together in the comfy chairs by the windows.

"Wow, what a view! It's so beautiful out there. We definitely have to find some time to go out there together," he said, staring out the window. I was thrilled to know that we were both thinking the same thoughts about the garden. "We'll do dinner tonight, drink a lot of wine, then go out into the gardens tonight under the moonlight. What do you think, babe, sound like a perfect night to you?"

"Absolutely," I answered, knowing that this was going to be an amazing night of love and romance, moonlight and lovemaking. I could feel all the anxiety and nervousness leaving my body and thoughts of my family at home seemed a million miles away.

We had a cigarette and talked about how his day with work went. I hung onto every word he spoke, all the while he was brushing my leg with his finger. It felt as though there had been no time or distance between us all these years. It was if he had just come home and was talking to me as naturally about his day as any couple would. I talked about my drive to the hotel and how I really loved being away from my "normal" routine. He smiled at me while I spoke - the same smile I'd always remembered.

"This is so weird, John. It feels like we've always been together and never spent any time apart," I said to him, staring deep into his eyes while I said it.

"I know, right? It feels like a normal day that I worked and came home to tell you all about it. I sure don't feel like a guy who's about to do something he shouldn't," he joked, but I know what he meant because

I felt the same way. How does anyone feel so calm when they're about to commit a mortal sin?

I don't know how, but I knew we were doing it and doing it quite well, I might add.

"I need to get out of this suit. Why don't you come down to my room with me while I change and then we can head out for a nice, long dinner. Sound good?" he asked, already undoing his tie and top button of his shirt.

"Sure, let me grab my hoodie and my pocketbook," I answered.

John laughed when he saw me grab my red sweatshirt.

"What? What's so funny," I asked, wondering why he was laughing at me.

"I'm not laughing at you, babe, I'm laughing because I have a red sweatshirt, too!" he said with a laugh. Once he said that, I started laughing, too. "And I'm wearing jeans and a white t-shirt to dinner as well!" Great minds think alike, I thought, and we both sat there laughing together.

"Oh, God, we're gonna look like twins!" I joked back at him.

"Eh, who cares, babe? Let's hit my room and get outta this hotel. What do you say?" he said, not really asking, but telling me as he took my hand in his and we began to leave my room.

I grabbed my sweatshirt and pocketbook and we left, hand in hand. We got down to his room, went inside and I sat down on the chair. John started undressing right in front of me and I could feel myself getting nervous again. I needed a few drinks before I could commit adultery. Doesn't everyone?

Yet as fast as he took his suit off, his jeans and a cute white t-shirt were on, the red sweatshirt completing his outfit. My fears were subsiding and I was beginning to feel much more comfortable in this situation.

"Ready for dinner? I'm starved! I found a quaint little restaurant in town for dinner. Hope you like it," he said, once again taking my hand in his.

"Anything is fine, John, I'm not really that hungry," I said, although I was starving! Just like a woman on a first date: never eat a lot in front of them or they'll think you're an expensive date!

I took his hand and off we went. We took his rental car and headed down to the town of Kennett Square to the local Inn. It was located in the historic section of town and was nothing short of charming. We walked in and found two sides to the restaurant: the pub side, which was casual, and the dining side, which was a bit more formal. We chose the pub side and were seated at a table next to the fireplace. There was a small bar filled with about ten men, which John and I dubbed "the good 'ol boys," wondering what they were doing out at night without their wives!

The waitress took our drink order: White Zinfandel for both of us. She brought the drinks and I was forever grateful for how fast she brought them. I definitely needed a drink right about now. I drank it down quickly, hoping he wouldn't notice, but I was feeling much more calm by the time I drank it, which is why I ordered another one right after.

"Don't get too drunk on me," John said, looking into my eyes with a somewhat "bad boy" tone to his voice. "I have plans for us tonight," he said as he winked at me. I was loving this more than I had imagined.

"Not to worry, two is my limit. And it won't make me drunk, just puts me in a mellow mood. This way you'll definitely be able to have your way with me later," I joked with him. Hell, he could have his way with me with no drink! Yet at the same time I couldn't believe I had said that to him. I was beginning to think I should forget the "two drink" limit and push it to three.

It was an amazing dinner and I couldn't decide if the food was that delicious or if it was because it had been so long since someone else cooked for me! John had the steak tartare and I had filet mignon accompanied with rosemary potatoes and steamed broccoli. It was absolutely delicious!

We finished our meal with coffee, his with cream and three sugars, just like I had remembered, and mine with Bailey's Irish Cream! I was feeling no pain, and definitely no inhibition, worries or guilt.

"Ready to go, babe?" he asked.

"Absolutely," I answered.

He paid the check, and we walked hand in hand over the cobblestone sidewalk to the car. He opened the door for me and helped me in. Damn, I thought, bucket seats! Times sure have changed since we were younger and dating in a car with a bench seat. Unless I wanted to straddle a console and stick shift, there'd be no sliding in next to him, but once he got in it was okay, because he placed his hand on my inner thigh, and that was the next best thing to a car with a bench seat.

I thought we were off to the Station House but John wasn't going our usual way. He seemed to be heading to the beach.

"Hey, what's the deal? We've got a prom to go to, in case you forgot, and we're supposed to be meeting Colleen and Frank at the bar before we go," I said feeling a bit annoyed. We were all dressed up and I sure didn't want to disrupt the look that took me hours to achieve if only to go on a jaunt to the beach!

"Babe, do you trust me?" he asked, placing a firm hand on my thigh.

"Yeah, you know I do, but what…" I tried to say, but was cut off by John…

"Just stop talking. Don't ask me questions. I love you and we're going to the beach for a bit. I have a little surprise for you, okay?" he said firmly.

"Okay, fine, anything you say," I said and now I really was feeling annoyed. My God, I thought, we're dressed to the nines here and not sticking to the plans.

"Good, that's my girl," he said calmly, placing his hand gently on top of mine. Once any part of his body connected to mine I was automatically calm. And then he did the inevitable, he brought my hand up to his mouth and kissed the top of it.

That got me every single time.

We drove to the beach in Spring Lake and pulled into a spot. He told me to close my eyes until he told me to open them.

"Are you kidding me? John, what the hell is going on?" I said, wondering what he was doing.

"Yes, my love, close your eyes, and no, I'm not kidding you, not this time. Now, for once, stop talking and do what I'm begging you to do!" he taunted.

"Fine, my eyes are closed," I said as I pressed my eyelids tightly shut, all the while hoping that I wasn't messing up my make-up that took me hours to do.

I heard some noise from the trunk but since I loved surprises, I kept my eyes closed. It felt like they were closed for an eternity, yet it was only a few minutes.

He came to my side of the car and said, "Now, keep them closed and let me help you out of the car."

He grabbed my hand, held up the bottom of my gown so I could get out, and gently guided me out of the car. He walked me just a step or two, and said, "Okay, baby, open your eyes."

My heart was beating so fast that I thought it would come right out of my chest, yet when he said to open my eyes, I did. And what I saw before me would live in my memory for the rest of my life.

There were candles lit in a half moon shape with white rose petals sprinkled all around and inside of them. It was absolutely beautiful! His placement of the candles matched the half moon shining above us and the sounds of the waves breaking on the shore was the music.

"Oh my God, John, what is this? It's beautiful!" I said, knowing full well that my eyes were tearing up and at that point I didn't care what my make-up would look like.

"This is a special night for us and I wanted to make it even more special. Now, step inside and wait just one more minute," he said as he guided me into the half moon circle of candles. I stood there as he ran back to the car. Suddenly, I heard music coming from the speakers in the car and "our song" by Meatloaf was playing. He walked over to me and took both of my hands in his.

"I fell in love with you at the mall that night when this song was playing and I'm even more in love with you now. You are my love, my life, my everything. Now, before we go to prom, I have to ask you something important. Will you marry me?" he said, not one ounce of nervousness in his voice.

Holy shit, was this really happening? Oh my God, Oh my God, someone pinch me, I thought! This was everything I ever dreamed of, except that it came sooner than I ever thought it would.

"John," I said, *looking into his eyes, eyes that were starting to look nervous waiting for an answer. "Yes, yes, yes, yes I'll marry you! Oh my God!" I almost screamed. Now I knew I had tears falling down my face.*

"Whew, I was afraid you were going to say no for a minute there, or worse, say that you had to think about it," he said with a sigh of relief. "I don't have a real engagement ring yet, but I have a "pre-engagement ring" for you, which means I will be engaged to you. Hope that's okay with you, babe," he said, and with that he pulled out a small gold ring with a diamond chip in it. He slid it on my finger, kissed the top of it, and said, "I love you. I love you so much. You're the one. You're "my" only one!" And with that, I saw a tear fall from his eye and then another tear after that.

"We're gonna have the best life together, babe, I promise," he said, his head now buried into my chest with sheer happiness.

"I know, my love, I know," I whispered to him as I kissed the top of his head.

Oh, my God, please don't let this be a dream…

Chapter 6

My mind was racing to a night back home. Richie had gotten laid off from his job just two short months ago, yet it felt as if it were a lifetime ago. The depression he was battling for the months prior to that seemed to only get worse with the loss of his job. It was a terrible shot in his ego, which was inflated to begin with. Yet it hit my husband incredibly hard - he'd been with this company for over 15 years. He had given his heart and soul to them, working endless numbers of hours and going on countless business trips which took him away from our family for weeks at a time. Little did I know then that these business trips were far more than "business," but I didn't care. I had my children and turned a blind eye to his "over-time hours" and trips for work.

Now he'd suffered the ultimate blow: the company no longer needed him, but we did, except his depression kept him from ever noticing that. The truth was and always will be that we were never the ones he wanted to be needed by. We were slowly, day by day, becoming his burden. His depression was becoming a black cloud over our home and our lives, and I could see his depression becoming ours.

For now, here we were, at The Meritage, my favorite restaurant, celebrating his new job. He was soaring higher than a kite, and if this is what Cloud Nine looked like, I could only imagine Heaven. This new company had sought him out and he felt like a whole man once again. He was needed. I was happy for him but I wondered why "our" needing him wasn't enough, why "our" needing him wasn't even a concern or priority. Well, enough with my thoughts, tonight was a celebration and

I wasn't about to spoil it by overanalyzing the situation, as I'm known to do much too often.

I decided to have a few drinks to put me in that hazy and happy mood. A couple glasses of wine and I'd be feeling nice and mellow, and hopefully wouldn't be thinking the thoughts that I was. We toasted his new success and ordered dinner. Salmon for him, filet mignon for me. He chatted endlessly throughout the dinner, bragging incessantly about how this company needed him, how badly they wanted him. I sat there as if I were a single member of the audience watching a one man Broadway show. I'm sure that if I would have spoken he wouldn't have even heard me. Sadly, that's how our marriage had become over the years. The world revolved around him, my life revolved around my children, and no one revolved around me. He kept talking so much that at some point I didn't remember anything he was saying. I had morphed into another place and that place was the one where I so wanted to be at that moment, at every moment of every day. That place was in John's arms.

"To hell with them. They're gonna miss me soon enough and I can sit back and laugh knowing that they screwed themselves by laying me off," he boasted. He really did take a twisted sort of pleasure in thinking of others' pain, although the reality was that we both knew he was damn lucky to have gotten this job. Yet he continued his sadistic sounding bragging.

I was worried about him. Sure, he was on a high right now, manic if you will, but I know that these moods of grandeur didn't last long. I knew that in time he'd wake up one morning and not be able to get out of bed. I was concerned about his well being, but I was more concerned about the future of our children and of my future with John.

"Yeah, this job sure is great. My new boss is terrific! He's about our age and a really smart guy. Very talented. I have a feeling that we'll be good friends down the line. Hey, maybe we should have him and his wife over for dinner sometime soon. Then we can all meet and I'll have my foot in the door even more for a promotion," he bragged. God, everything was always about him and what he could gain from everyone else.

"Sure, that'd be great. Just let me know when," I answered, not really too interested in the conversation or having two strangers over for dinner. The last thing I wanted was to have to spruce up my whole house to impress some snooty boss and his wife and I certainly didn't want to be the pawn in my husband's plight to impress his boss.

Yet, as always, he expected me to act and behave as he wanted, and as always, I would do it. He wanted a trophy wife, the perfect little hostess, and would surely start getting me ready days before this dinner by telling me how to behave and what to say. It was daunting.

The sad thing is that over time I had learned to become the woman he wanted, and long ago I had forgotten the woman I really was. It was John who was reintroducing me to my old self, the girl he had fallen in love with so many years ago, and the girl who I was beginning to remember. He could always make me remember, yet once I left the safety of his arms, I quickly forgot all about that girl. I forgot who she was and how much I had missed her.

"Oh and hey, hon, did I tell you that this guy went to the same high school you did?" he asked, still not piquing my curiosity. I could have cared less.

"Nope, you didn't tell me that. You've told me everything else, but you didn't tell me that," I said quite sarcastically, almost sounding bored. "What's his name?" I asked, deciding it was easier to go along with this charade than fight it.

I picked up my glass of wine and took a large gulp just as my husband said his name.

"It's Johnny Davis." Holy shit!

At that moment I began to choke on the mouthful of wine that was just beginning to go down my throat when he told me. I took another gulp, much bigger than the last, to try and help myself stop choking, but several more loud, gasping coughs ensued.

"Are you okay?" my husband asked, looking around to see who was looking at his wife making a scene. I could see the embarrassment on his face. Forget the fact that I was shocked, it was always about how things looked to everyone else, and more importantly, how HE looked.

"Sure, I'm okay now," I sputtered in between the last few coughs. I quickly drank down the last bit of wine, signaled the waiter for yet another glass, and lit a cigarette.

"You know I hate that, don't you? You're a mom, for Christ's sake, how stupid can you be? Why you ever started smoking again is beyond me," he droned on, and on, and on.

"And really, a THIRD glass of wine? Really?" he said in his usual condescending voice. "Do you really need to drink that much?"

Yes I do, I thought to myself. I should be drinking 24 hours a day, 7 days a week just to live with you, but as always, I succumbed to his tone and answered, "I know, it's just that it's a rare occasion that we're out without the kids and that we're even out at all," I said as the waiter answered my prayers with another glass. At that point I just wanted to tell him to bring the bottle.

"Gee, you mean you hate this? Who would have thought," I said sarcastically as I blew the smoke into his face. God, he could be such a pain in the ass at times. So righteous, yet he forgets all that he did as a teenager. He was the reason I started smoking again in the first place. It seemed to be the only way I could get his attention, albeit not the attention I was looking for.

"Anyway," he said, dismissing the apparent change in my mood," do you know him?"

"Yes, I know him" I answered quite matter of factly. Oh, yes, I most certainly do know him: he's my lover.

It was late at night when I wandered out onto my deck in my pajamas. I could hear the tree frogs in the woods harmonizing with an assortment of birds that were screeching as if the sun was about to rise. I sat down in my rocker and lit a cigarette. It was a bad habit I'd recently picked up again after many years, a habit which I had to keep well hidden from my children who were fast asleep. I knew it was a very unhealthy thing to be doing, but I found it to be quite calming and Lord knows that I need a sense of calm in my life these days. I also needed this type of night. A night of peace and quiet to think about what I was doing in my life and what I was doing TO my life. I needed to think about the love affair I was having.

My hand was shaking as I lit another cigarette.

I'd never planned on having an affair, never even dreamed of it, but here I was in the throes of one. I was totally dedicated to being a great mom to my children. I attended church every Sunday, believed in God and followed the Commandments as best I could, well, except for the occasional "taking the Lord's name in vain." I was certain God would forgive me for that. I wasn't so sure He'd forgive me for this affair, but I couldn't stop it. The truth of the matter was that I didn't want to stop it.

And that is my sin and my saving Grace all wrapped up in one.

So here I sit, staring up at the stars, wondering if my lover was doing the same, all the while contemplating what it was I was doing. I knew in my head that this affair was wrong. We were both married with children. Yet my heart couldn't accept that this was wrong. It felt so right. This wasn't the typical affair that "other" people have. This was a true love affair with my soul mate, the person whom I never stopped loving despite the fact that I was married to someone else. This was the man I always dreamed of spending the final days of my life with. No, this was much more than an affair. This was true love of the sweetest, purest kind. This was a love that would never and had never died throughout all these years.

My mind was awash with thoughts of whether to end it or keep it as it was with daily phone calls and emails.

I closed my eyes and as I leaned back into the seat, my mind took me back to our first email, the one that had changed my way of living, my way of being, forever.

I couldn't believe it. We're engaged! The prom seemed so much less important now. We spent a few more minutes at the beach, savoring this beautiful, romantic moment. I couldn't stop staring down at my left hand, at my "pre-engagment ring!" It was so perfectly sweet.

"How are you feeling, babe?" John asked as he grabbed my left hand and kissed the ring.

"I don't even know where to begin," I said, still shaking from the excitement and from the moment of knowing that I had just committed to marrying him.

"I've always wanted this. I've always known that I wanted to spend the rest of my life with you and now it's my dream turned into my reality. Is this really real?" I asked, looking deeply into his eyes.

"Oh, it's really real, alright. It's what I've always wanted, too, you and me, together forever," he said as he pulled me into his arms.

"I know that we have college ahead of us but the moment we graduate is the moment we get married. I'm not waiting one more minute for you to officially become Mrs. John Davis," he said as he kissed my forehead.

"John, I love you so much and I can't wait to marry you. Four years is going to seem like a lifetime," I said wanting to say "forget college, let's just get married now."

"The time will fly, babe, and at the end of those four years there will be two college degrees, a husband and wife," he said reassuringly. "Now, if I remember correctly, we have a prom to go to!" he joked.

"Yes we do and we have some news to share with everyone," I said excitedly.

We packed up the candles and got into the car.

My mind was in a blissful haze of love and of a future that was now promised to me, to us.

We got into the car, kissed each other and headed to the prom.

Chapter 7

We headed back to the hotel after a delicious dinner. I was definitely feeling relaxed and couldn't wait to get back to my room with him. The anticipation was building, as were some other things in my body. This man could turn on every switch in my body as if igniting a flame that had gone out long ago. I wanted him. I wanted him so badly and I had to believe that in an hour or two I would have him.

We drove back to the hotel, hand in hand, all the while talking and laughing. He intermittently would bring my hand to his lips to kiss it. It was incredibly erotic.

We pulled into the lot, parked the car and headed up to the room. The woman who usually sits behind the desk wasn't there and I was happy about that. The last thing I wanted right now was someone wasting my precious time chatting about nothing.

The elevator doors opened and in we went. He pressed our floor number and pushed his body into mind against the wall. I could feel his excitement through his pants and if he had put his hands down my pants he would have felt mine.

The doors opened and we almost raced down to the room. The moment we went inside is the moment that all our pent up excitement exploded. John pulled me in and started to undress me. He took off my hoodie and my shirt, then unbuttoned my pants and pulled them down to my ankles so that I could kick them off.

I slid off my bra and panties and he began to kiss my nipples. They became hard at the touch of his tongue but he didn't stay there long.

He slid it down my stomach, teasing my belly button and then slid it back up to my mouth to kiss me hard.

I began to undress him just as quickly as he had done to me. First his hoodie, his shirt, then his pants. I slid his boxers off and grabbed onto his excitement with my hand. He was as hard as a rock.

"John," was all I could say as I lost all of my senses.

"Shhh, don't talk," he said as he pushed me onto the bed. I lay there and he stood over me looking at me.

"You're beautiful," he said as he climbed onto the bed. He kissed me on the mouth and began to shower me with kisses down my entire body until he got to the area that would take me to a place that I'd never imagined that I could go to.

"Oh my God, I thought," as I closed my eyes and rolled back my head. I lay there enjoying each movement of his tongue until he thrust his finger deep inside of me, one orgasm after another.

Just as I was about to grab him he got on top of me and entered me. He felt amazing. He was so hard and I could feel every bit of him inside of me. He began to move slowly at first but I knew that he wasn't going to be able to hold out much longer.

Suddenly he began thrusting faster, harder and harder, deeper and deeper until sounds came from my throat and his that almost sounded primeval. We were intensely excited and in a split second we came... together.

He stayed inside of me for a few minutes before he rolled over and laid his head on my chest.

"Oh my God, that was incredible. Was it like that when we were in high school?" he asked as he reached for his cigarettes on the nightstand.

"If I remember correctly, it was pretty good in high school but this? This was something I never knew existed," I said as I took a cigarette from him.

We sat up in bed, both smoking and sitting in complete awe at what had just happened. Our bodies were wet with sweat and my mouth was as dry as cotton. I reached over to pour a glass of wine that I had left out before we went to dinner.

"Babe, wow, just wow," I said as I took a big gulp of wine.

"Wow is right," he said and with that we finished our cigarettes, turned off the lights, pulled up the covers and nestled into each other's arms.

We arrived at the prom in just a few minutes. The parking lot was riddled with everyone's parents' best cars. We found a spot and walked into the venue. The prom was in full swing with a live band playing music. Everyone seemed to be up on the dance floor. I guess we were a bit late to the show!

We stopped to have our prom pictures taken and walked in to find our table. It was near the band which would make it difficult to talk but we didn't care. Colleen and Frank saw us and waved us over!

"We're over here!" Colleen yelled.

I could tell that Frank and her already had a good buzz going. John and I would have to catch up but I would say we were already on a bit of a natural high from our engagement.

"You guys look awesome," she said.

"So do you!" I answered.

"What took you so long? I thought you were right behind us," Colleen said, taking a sip of her soda. I knew that it was spiked because we all snuck in rum and vodka.

"Give me a sip of your drink or get me one," I said, "and then I'll tell you."

John and Frank walked over to the bar to get a couple of sodas and came back with them. We very carefully reached into our pocketbooks to pull out the rum and vodka shooters we had snuck in and poured them into our glasses. I took a big sip of mine and John did as well.

The four of us sat down at the table for eight. Everyone else at our table was on the dance floor.

"So, why were you late?" Colleen asked.

I held up my left hand to show her.

"He asked me to marry him!" I said excitedly!

"What? Are you kidding me? Let me see that! Frank, look at this!" she signaled to Frank.

"You're engaged?" Frank said, looking at John as if to say "Really?"

"Yup, we are. John took me down to the beach and proposed. Can you believe it?

We're going to get married as soon as we're done with college," I said to Colleen. "And you just have to be my maid of honor!" I said to her.

"And I will!" she said back excitedly.

The four of us chatted for a few minutes and then decided to hit the dance floor. A slow song came on just as we went up to dance.

John pulled me close into him and kissed my neck.

"Just think, babe, in four years we'll be dancing like this as husband and wife, except you'll be in a wedding dress and I'll be in a much nicer tuxedo!" he joked.

"That's right, babe, that's right," I said as I nuzzled into his shoulder.

We danced the night away…

Right into the sunrise.

Chapter 8

I awoke in his arms as the sun peeked through a slender opening in the curtains. I curled into his back, closed my eyes and inhaled his scent, wanting to remember it forever. I could feel his heart beating in perfect rhythm with mine. It had only been hours before that I had surrendered myself to him, my body rising and falling in rhythm with his as he moved within me. Strange, I thought, he had been the main character of my fantasies all these months, yet it was no longer just a dream, it had become a reality, a permanent part of me. Our souls had utterly and totally connected and I was still feeling that connection now. I couldn't turn back now. Our love affair had become a sweet and beautiful truth that in time would sustain me through my every moment of every day.

He rolled over to face me and kissed me gently on the mouth, his tongue reaching for mine, finding it in an instant. Our mouths fit together like the pieces of a puzzle and I found great pleasure and happiness in the mere touch of his lips. Being with him was as natural as breathing. We awoke together, rising to full consciousness. It was time to dress and get ready for our last few hours together. We savored the moments in our room, dressing slowly as if to slow time.

We'd built our relationship over several months now. It had all started innocently enough - two old friends reconnecting through email - yet the truth of the matter was that he was not merely an old friend. We had been lovers throughout high school and into college. We had fallen in love instantly during our senior year of high school and realized in a short time that we were true soul mates. Sadly enough the relationship crumbled during college, yet here we are now, almost a quarter of a century later, realizing that the intense love we had felt for each other then was still very much alive now. We had merely tucked it away in our hearts for safe keeping.

What had started between us as a friendship had now grown into a love affair. Neither of us had been seeking this or had even planned on things happening the way that they did, but they did.

Sometimes our "morals" cannot sustain us through a feeling that is simply stronger and larger than life itself. There was such a deep love between us that we knew it must be bigger than anything we'd ever encountered before. We had no control over any of this, and if in fact we did, things would still have progressed to the point that they were at now.

So here we are, secret phone calls late at night, torrid emails by day, and now our first stolen trip away together. We had crossed the invisible line which exists in all marriages. It was our secret now and would most assuredly change our lives if it were ever uncovered.

There were many times that we both wondered how something so wrong could feel so right, making us feel whole and complete again for the first time in many years. Neither of us had the answers, but we could both agree that this was where we needed to be right now. Time would tell our story and hopefully provide us with an answer…

The prom was a success and the engagement was a triumph. Colleen, Frank, John and I left together and headed to Pat's Diner in Belmar, a place we always stopped at after being out at the bars. Here we were, dressed in prom attire, ordering a Jersey Shore staple: pork roll, egg and cheese on a hard roll. It was near one o'clock in the morning by the time we got to Pat's and most of our class was here as well.

Our good friend, Steve McRae, was there as well. His mom was a waitress here and always graciously waited on "us kids," as she would say. She was a hard worker and we loved it when our table got her as our waitress. We always wondered if she secretly planned to have us seated at one of her tables.

"So, kids, how was the prom," she said as she held her order pad. "Everyone have a good time?"

"It was awesome, Mrs. McRae. We had a great time!" we all answered.

"Anything good happen?" she asked while intermittently taking our orders and writing them down.

"We got engaged," John said as he grabbed my hand and held it up to show her the ring.

"Well look at that! Congratulations! That calls for a little something special after you eat your breakfast," she said jokingly, all the while knowing that a run at Pat's Diner was a sure way to help you sober up before you went home.

"Thanks, Mrs. McRae," we said and she was off to the kitchen to give them our order.

We chatted at the table, talking about the events of the evening and more importantly, of our engagement.

"So, let's talk about this wedding," Colleen said.

"What kind of dress do you want? Big wedding or small? What color for the bridesmaids?" she said as if she were more excited than me.

"Geez, I don't know. I haven't even told my parents yet," I said.

"Well, we can still talk about it," she said.

"Okay, beautiful white dress, small wedding and lavender for the bridesmaids dresses," I said as if I had already thought about that day and truth be told, I had a million times.

"Really, lavender?" she said.

"Yes, really, but it's still four years away!" I said.

Mrs. McRae was walking out from the kitchen with our sandwiches. She placed our plates in front of us.

"I'll be right back with something special!" she said so sweetly.

We started to eat and within a minute she walked over with a heart shaped pancake topped with strawberries and whipped cream.

"Just a little something for the happy couple!" she said with a twinkle in her eye.

"Oh my gosh, thank you so much! I love it!" I said as I leaned towards John to kiss his cheek.

"Mrs. McRae, you're the best. You know we love you! " John said.

"Yes I am and yes I do!" she joked back as she walked to the next table filled with more kids from the prom.

We must have sat there an hour together, eating our breakfast and all four of us digging into that heart shaped pancake.

It was certainly a night to remember.

We paid the check, said our goodbyes and headed back to my parents house.

It was late and John stayed over. We slept on the couch, he at one end and me at the other.

I couldn't wait until morning to tell my parents.

Chapter 9

The minutes sped by quickly and it was time, all too soon, to leave the room where we'd spent the last several days together. It was our secret chamber in which the real world could not penetrate. We'd decided to spend our last few hours together outside in a nearby garden. It would be a beautiful ending to a special time together, one which I had hoped would leave an impression on our minds not of sadness in saying goodbye, but in happiness of knowing that we had become one in the most intimate way that one could. We had given ourselves to each other completely, body and soul. Neither time nor distance could or would ever erase that.

We each took our own cars to the gardens. The day was warm and the sky clear and blue, not a trace of a cloud. We strolled together, hand in hand, never wanting to let go of one another, especially at this moment knowing that our time was fleeting, with no promise of a "next time."

In a few short hours we would be back in our respective lives miles apart, worlds apart for that matter, yet for now we clung to this precious time together as a child clings to its most cherished toy, never wanting to let go of it, never wanting to share it.

Silence enveloped us as we walked. The gardens were bursting with bright, brilliant colors and the air was filled with the musical sounds of the birds. The fragrance of the flowers was intoxicating at best and I thought to myself that at this moment we were as close to Heaven as we would ever get. The touch of his hand intertwined with mine. It felt as sweet as candy and as pure as spring water. I couldn't imagine being any happier.

The minutes passed more quickly than we would have liked and we knew that the inevitable good-bye would shortly be upon us. The sun warmed my skin as my intense love for him grew even warmer. It filled my heart with such abundance that at times it felt as though it may burst. Maybe it already had because every inch of my body felt alive when I was with him. It was as though there was a piece of him in every ounce of my being. He had filled all the gaps and I felt whole again in knowing that now he was a part of me.

We sat down on a bench surrounded by bushes of beautiful pink and red roses. How fitting for such a moment! He placed his arm gently around my shoulder and I rested my head on his. A flock of birds flew overhead startling us out of our trance. He looked down at me and gazed into my eyes, taking my face into both of his hands.

"I love you," he whispered to me, and a long, passionate kiss followed before I could respond.

"I love you, too," I answered, hoping that he knew the depth of my words. He was my other life, all of it. I was his completely, body and soul.

A few clouds began to fill the blue sky and the sun tucked behind a cloud and the breeze which once blew warm was now turning cool. We knew it was time to go. It was time to say good-bye until another circumstance could steal us away for another time together. We both knew the risks and restrictions of our relationship, our "affair," yet we also knew of the intense love and attraction that existed between us, one that neither time, distance nor circumstance would ever be able to destroy. Perhaps it was because the reality was that we wouldn't let it. We were true romantics, believing that we were in the place together that we had been moving towards all of our lives.

The hour of separation had arrived and we walked together slowly toward our cars. The silence was deafening. Our mouths met to form one last kiss, the kiss that would last for what seemed an eternity. His tongue met mine for the last time and I savored the taste of him. All too soon our lips parted and a tear rolled down my cheek, a tear that he immediately kissed away. We embraced one last time, committing to memory the feeling of our bodies pressed together. A few drops of rain began to sprinkle down upon us and with that we knew it was time to say good-bye.

We got into our cars, waving good-bye as we drove away. Tears began to flow heavily from my eyes and the ache in my heart was unbearable. I wondered if he was feeling the same way. In just a few short days my life had changed completely. I was no longer the person I once was and I knew in my heart that I never would be again. I belonged to him forever. Nothing would be able to tear us apart now. We had arrived at the place we had been searching for all our lives and had arrived at our final destination…a life together.

"I guess the prom was good?" I heard my Dad say as he startled us out of sleep.

"Geez, Pop, what time is it?" I asked in a sleepy tone of voice.

"It's time that you both get up. Mom has coffee in the kitchen. Let's move it along," he said with a tone of annoyment in his voice at seeing his daughter and her boyfriend sleeping together on the couch.

"Okay," I said as he walked into the kitchen. I nudged John to wake up.

"What happened?" he said in a groggy voice.

"Well, my dad just caught us sleeping together on the couch!" I joked back.

"Oh, shit," he said. "I'm gonna get it now."

"Nah, I don't think so but we better get up and go have coffee with them. Are we going to tell them?"

"Coffee, first, babe and I'll let you know," he said as he threw the blanket off of himself, sat up and looked at himself and then at me.

"God, we're still in our prom clothes! I definitely need coffee," he said.

We got up and went into the kitchen to find my mom having her coffee with a cigarette and my dad drinking his while watching our black and white television in the kitchen.

"Morning," we both said.

"Well good morning," they said.

"I'll get you coffee," my mom said as she got up and poured two cups for us.

We sat down at the table with them.

"How was the prom?" they asked.

"It was great! Hung out with Colleen and Frank and had a really good time. Danced all night!" I said.

"You sat with Colleen?" my mom asked with a look on her face.

Colleen and I were best friends and my mom always thought she was a bad influence on me but it was never true. Colleen and I had a great friendship and didn't "always" get in trouble but if we did, it was both of us and neither of our mothers saw it that way. Each mom blamed the other one's daughter!

"Yes, she's my best friend," I said slightly annoyed.

"Whatever, did you have a good time?" she asked, giving up on the "Colleen" thing.

"We had a great time, didn't we, John?" I asked with a slight kick to his foot as if to say "Are you going to tell them?"

"Yup, it was fun," he said, just like that.

I looked at him in disbelief. Seriously, mister, we just got engaged and you're not going to tell them?

We finished our coffee and John gathered his things to go home and sleep for the rest of the day. I walked out with him to his car.

"What was that? Why didn't you say anything to them?" I asked, feeling a bit annoyed.

"Because your father just found us sleeping on the couch and seemed annoyed. I didn't think that telling him I was marrying his daughter was appropriate at that moment. Okay?" he asked. He was hungover, I could tell, and I was as well.

"You're right, I get it," I said as I kissed him goodbye.

"Get some sleep, babe, I'll call you later," he said as he got into his car.

"Love you," I said as I kissed him goodbye.

"Love you, too, and remember...you're engaged!" he said with a smile as he drove off.

I walked back into the house and up to my room. I peeled off my prom clothes, put on my pajamas and went back to bed.

This sleep would surely be filled with good dreams.

And all of them would be about John.

Chapter 10

The two hour drive back home seemed to take an eternity and all I could do was think of John. My eyes were burning and my stomach hurt. I felt so sick. My mind kept playing the details of our lovemaking over and over again and I couldn't stop thinking about him. I was sure my stomach hurt from guilt, Gods' subtle way of punishing me for my adultery, yet I realized that this feeling wasn't guilt, it was fear. Fear of losing him, of not knowing if he'd feel so guilty when he got home that he'd end everything. I was fearful of not knowing if he truly loved me, fear of not knowing when or if I'd ever see him again. All of these feelings were unfamiliar to me - I didn't know what to do with them or how to handle them. I was feeling completely overwhelmed.

Before long I found myself turning down my street with the familiar sight of my home and the kids' bikes and soccer balls strewn across the lawn. There I was, pulling into the driveway about to walk into the home where my husband and children were, knowing I could never share any of these thoughts and feelings with them. I'd have to lie about my trip. I'd have to act calm, even though my insides were churning with sadness. I need to go into the house and resume my role of wife and mother. The part of mother would be easy but the part of wife would be a completely different story.

I didn't feel like his wife anymore, not that I really had in years, but now I held a secret. For the first time in my marriage I lied and had a secret bigger than any I could have ever imagined.

I'd given my body and soul to the one man I truly loved, had always loved, and he felt more like a husband to me than my own did.

I felt such happiness and wholeness since we had made love, yet now my heart was aching. "This affair is going to kill me," I thought, "how am I ever going to accept the fact that he's going home to her when I know in my heart it should be me."

I wondered if he felt the same way towards his wife that I was feeling towards my husband. I wondered if he still kissed her and told her that he loved her. I wondered if he would make love to her tonight, only hours after making love to me.

My mind was racing to places I didn't want it to go, and all I could think of as I was about to walk into the house was "what made him want me at all?"

A few weeks had passed and we still hadn't told my parents of our engagement. I was feeling a bit nervous as to why John wouldn't want to tell them. We were so happy and yet, without telling my parents, it didn't seem real. He hadn't even told his parents. I wondered why this was.

And then it was Saturday Night date night.

John picked me up. He didn't come to the door as he usually did but honked the horn instead. I heard it and went outside to get in the car.

I opened the door and slid in the door across the bench seat. I kissed him gently on the cheek and he drove off.

"Babe, what's going on?" I asked, getting the feeling that something was wrong.

"Nothing, why?" he answered with a tone in his voice that let me know that he knew what was wrong.

"You asked me to marry you and we haven't told our parents," I answered, as if demanding for a reason why he hadn't.

"Listen, we're just 18 years old and if we told our parents that we got engaged they'd have a fit. You know that," he said, sounding annoyed.

"Okay, I get that, but we ARE engaged. You asked me to marry you. It's not like we're doing it tomorrow. We're planning on doing it after college. What's the problem?" I asked.

"The problem is that I don't want to hear shit from either of our parents. Can't we just keep it to ourselves and our friends? Why do you have to let

everyone know? Why do our parents have to know? Why?" he asked. I knew then and there that there was a problem.

"Because, John, we made a commitment to each other. You asked me to marry you and I said yes and why wouldn't we tell our parents? We're not planning on doing it until after college and that's four years away?" I answered expecting a decent answer.

"I don't need a hard time from anyone. I don't need your parents or mine telling me that we're too young," he answered angrily.

"Your parents would be fine with this and mine would, too. We're waiting to get married, why would they give us a hard time? We just made a commitment for our wedding to happen in four years, not today," I answered, quite logically I might add.

"No. We're not telling them. It's one thing telling our friends, it's another telling our parents. We're not doing it," he said as if he controlled what I did.

Truth is, he did control me.

And we didn't tell our parents.

And we never did get married after college.

Chapter 11

My mind kept racing with thoughts of the time that we had just spent together. I decided to get a glass of wine, or two or three, to keep me company this late at night on my deck. The kids and my husband were asleep, so all my secrets were safe outside with me.

The first glass of wine went down quickly and the second did too. I could feel it doing just what I had hoped it would. My body was becoming relaxed and my mind was feeling calm.

The fear of this affair was leaving my thoughts and the beauty and excitement of it were entering them.

I closed my eyes as if to see our last day together replay itself like a movie. I took a deep breath and remembered even more...

All of these thoughts are what had taken me outside to escape into this beautiful, balmy spring night. I need to think about this. Most days are good and it's all so easy to handle. Some days aren't so good and the fear of losing him weighs terribly heavy on me. For now this affair seems as if it's the right thing for me to do. John's always there for me, good days or bad. He listens, he cares and more importantly, he loves me. At this time in my life this affair seems right, it's what I need to do, what I need to do for me, that is. It's all very simple in the end: I love him, he loves me. Time will tell our story and we'll keep loving each other right through it.

At least I hoped that we would.

I was feeling terribly sleepy now after three glasses of wine and decided it best to get some sleep. Sleep is the one place that I could always find John. He was in every dream and they made me feel like I was really with him.

I trekked up the stairs quietly, so as not to wake the kids or my husband, who had taken to sleeping alone in one of our spare bedrooms. That worked for me. I opened the bedroom door, shutting it lightly, and slid into bed. I was asleep in minutes and I know that because John was with me and dreams of our last day together were once again in my mind, even as I slept.

The weeks passed after the prom and John and I had still not told my parents about our engagement. I was upset about it at first but as time passed it bothered me less and less. I knew we were engaged and so did all of our friends. Maybe that's all that really mattered.

Still, it didn't seem "real" without telling them.

Time was moving at a fast pace and our graduation day from high school was just a few short weeks away.

We were deep into our senior year of high school and getting ready for college. Weekend nights were spent at the Station House with our friends and drinking in our cars at the beach. Weeknights were spent studying for our upcoming finals.

John and I were still deeply in love, but something felt off. I couldn't quite put my finger on it but that gut feeling was there.

It was a feeling that the closer it got to going off to college, the further away it was for our wedding day.

I tried many times to talk to John about it but it was of no use, he was not going to have any conversation concerning our engagement.

I tried my hardest to believe that everything was okay, that this was just pre-final jitters and nervousness over leaving for college in a few short months.

But I knew in my heart that nothing was okay.

The love of my life was hiding something or running from something.

I often wondered if it was ME that he was running from.

Time would eventually answer the questions.

Chapter 12

I was thankful to have this road trip today. I had been home for over a week now, and while my heart ached for John, I knew my soul needed an afternoon with my oldest and dearest girlfriend, Colleen. So I grabbed a coffee and my cigarettes and headed to Delaware for an afternoon of girl talk, advice, and anxiety.

My anxiety was at an all time high keeping my dark secret buried within my heart. Secrets of guilt, sin, and the best love and sex I've ever had. God I hoped that Colleen had the answers for me, or at least had the questions to ask me.

Colleen and I had known each other as far back as grade school, but it wasn't until high school that we became "soul sisters." She was my best friend and still is. We've certainly had our ups and downs, not speaking much for years at a time, yet in the end she's the only one I trust with my deepest and darkest secrets…and with my affair.

I remember when I first got to know her - she was a wonder to me! She took chances and wasn't afraid of anything. She was the popular and outgoing girl while I was the shy and introverted one. She was all the things I wasn't, and maybe that was the attraction I felt at first meeting her. I felt as if being close to her would allow me insight into what it was like to be "somebody." As luck would have it, we became best friends, spending all our free time together, at least until we reached the age of having a boyfriend. We had an unspoken rule that "boyfriends come first." We knew our friendship could withstand being on the back burner.

We spent our summer days on the beach in Manasquan, greasing ourselves with Ban du Soleil Gelee #4, slurping down Gee-Gee's famous "Lem-Teas and lunching on frozen yogurt with granola. She taught me how to smoke and how to inhale. We were together through the broken hearts of our first loves and she was there to listen to the details of the night I lost my virginity.

We worked together during our senior year of high school at the Holiday House on the New Jersey Parkway, she on the day shift, me on the night. We met on weekend nights after work to go to the local movie theater in Belmar to see the "Rocky Horror Picture Show." As we grew into legal age we went to all the bars together, me sitting on the barstool in the hopes of meeting my future husband, she on the dance floor in the hopes of finding a good time.

I was there when the love of her life was killed in a tragic car accident and she was there when my grandmother passed away. We were each other's maid of honor and were there through our numerous pregnancies, morning sickness and swelling, and shared our "war stories" of our childbirths. She was my wild side and even at our age now, it was no exception.

She had been through an affair and "knew the ropes." This was my first, and hopefully, my last. Today's lunch with her would be my confessional over John and our affair. I knew I could tell Colleen anything and if there's one thing I knew for certain about her was that she would be honest with me. No matter what transpired over the years of our friendship her ability to be honest with me always remained. Well, almost. She never shared her affair with me often, mainly because she felt that I was judgemental. I can look back now and see that I was. I wanted everyone to live as I did: married, happily or not, following the Ten Commandments, not breaking the rules and staying true to the family. And most importantly, putting yourself on the bottom rung of the ladder because everyone was more important than yourself.

Never say never.

My mantra now is "Be careful how you judge people because inevitably it will come back to bite you in the proverbial ass." How true that is now. There isn't anyone who knows me that would ever think I would be capable of having an affair.

Yet here I was.

As human beings I believe that given a circumstance in which we feel as though we're nothing, we become capable of just about anything.

I arrived at Colleen's house two hours later. She took me to a quaint little town on the Chesapeake Bay for lunch. We ordered salads and she ordered a glass of wine.

"For God's sake, order a damn drink!" she ordered me, quite firmly I might add. "You won't be driving home for a few hours and by then you'll be fine. We definitely need drinks today. I want to hear the whole story about you and John and I know a few glasses of wine will make you spill it a lot easier and quicker. Now, order the damn drink already!" I love this woman. What would I do without a friend like her? At this moment I couldn't imagine.

"Okay, okay, but I'll be able to tell you everything without a drink. I'm in love with him, I don't think I ever stopped loving him, and I want to be with him. I can't stop thinking about him. I still can't believe that I cheated! I can't believe that I crossed the line but I haven't felt that good or safe in a million years. We made love as though we were made for each other - we are a perfect fit. There, see, I could say it all without a drink," I said, knowing that now that I said it outloud to her I really did need that drink.

"Don't think about the moral thing right now. I've known you forever and you've loved this guy forever. You talked about him all throughout your marriage, shit, I'm surprised you didn't name one of your kids after him," she laughed as she waved down the waiter for another round.

"Have sex with him, but don't put any expectations or rules on him. Guys hate that and remember, YOU'RE not his wife. He gets that at home. Don't be needy, don't act jealous, don't give him any reason to think that you're a burden or a pain in the ass and he won't leave you. Then, you can still love him, have sex with him, and carry on with your life as normal," she said very matter-of-factly, taking a bite of her salad as if she had just filled me in about the latest PTA meeting.

God, I thought to myself, is there a rule book of affairs that I don't know about? And if these ARE the rules, they suck. John and I weren't like this, it wasn't just about sex. We were about love, we were in love, we made love. I couldn't imagine him ever thinking I was a burden to him in any way, but I'll be honest, Colleen now had my mind wandering.

She ordered a third drink and I still nursed my first. She proceeded to tell me her "affair" story and I was grateful to hear about it. We laughed and giggled over lunch just like we did when we were in high school.

And I have to say that it felt so good to feel a little bit "bad" again.

It'd been a long time since I had allowed my mind and my thoughts to wander outside of the perimeter of "wife and mother." For the first time in a long time it felt like "me" again, laughing like I hadn't in years, saying things that I had forgotten I even had thought about, and enjoying the company of my oldest, bestest friend. I was already starting to feel sad over having to leave and go home soon. I hated living so far away from her.

I hoped that all these changes in my life wouldn't destroy me.

We lingered over lunch and strolled through the town. It was starting to get late and I knew I needed to get home. We drove back to her house to have a last cup of coffee together.

"Listen, don't think about it so much, but definitely be careful. You could easily get hurt in this relationship because nothing can come of it. He'll never leave his wife and I doubt very much that you'll leave your husband, so just be happy with seeing him when you can. Don't, I repeat, don't start to need him. I care about you and he hurt you a long time ago. Keep it simple and be careful. There's nothing like wild sex with a lover. Enjoy yourself and do it for YOU for a change," she said as though she were my life coach and truth be told, maybe she was.

It meant the world to me for her to take the time to give me her "words of wisdom" but I didn't have the heart to tell her that I already do need him, that I already do want him, and that I would, in fact, most definitely leave my husband for him if he asked me to.

"I gotta go," I said. "It's getting late and I can only imagine what my house looks like by now."

"Well, don't lose the directions to my house. I expect to see you here more often. When you need to run away from home, run here," she said as she hugged and kissed me good-bye.

"Don't worry, I'll be back. I had a great time and being away for a long day felt great," I said as I walked out the front door. I got into my car and waved good-bye as I drove off. The sun was beginning to set and it was getting darker with each minute. I turned on the radio and an Anita Baker song was playing. The lyrics were imprinting themselves onto my mind and all I could hear was the sultry and smooth voice singing: "What have you done to me? I can't eat, I cannot sleep. I'm not the same anymore..." This was my life with John in a nutshell.

And only time would tell where we would go...

John and Frank went surfing for the day so Colleen and I decided to make a day of it. We grabbed our beach chairs, sunscreen and cigarettes, and headed to Manasquan beach where, as always, we parked ourselves right in front of Gee-Gees.

Once we got our Lem-Teas we sat down and grabbed out the latest books we were reading. I turned on my small radio and we relaxed into our chairs under blue skies and a tanning index of 10! It was the perfect day.

"I'm glad the boys are off surfing. I don't mind watching John but it gets boring after a while. I'm just sitting there by myself," I said to Colleen, almost whining.

"I hear 'ya," she said, "same with Frank. It's good for us all to take a break once in a while."

"We're all going out tonight, right?" I asked.

"Yeah, I think the boys wanted us to go to Park Place in Asbury Park. There's a good Southern rock band playing," she said without looking up from her book.

"I'm good with that," I said.

"Should we grab dinner first?" she asked.

"No, I'll eat home. You know that we'll end up at Pat's Diner when the bar closes.

"You're right about that!" she said.

We spent the next few glorious hours enjoying the beach and some time without the boys. A few more drinks and a frozen yogurt with granola and we were ready to go home.

Our skin was bright red from the sun and I just knew we'd be feeling the "burn" later that night, but we didn't care. We were about to graduate high school and head off to college. We were all going far away from each other so it makes days like this with your best friend even more special.

We packed up our stuff and headed to her car, a lime green Vega. She dropped me off at my parents house and said, "See 'ya in a few hours! Wear something sexy tonight!"

"I will, no worries. I'll even wear my spikiest heels!" I joked back and with that she was off.

Now to shower and get ready for a night on the town with my love.

I hope he'll be okay tonight.

Chapter 13

Thank God for a Monday morning. I love the weekends but I do look forward to Monday mornings when the kids go back to school and Richie goes back to work. The routine is restored back into my life and I feel so much less stress that way. By nine o'clock the last of the kids are out of the door and onto the bus, only the youngest is left home with a cold and he's one of the easiest of my kids.

I put a Disney movie on the television for him and poured myself a hot cup of coffee. This is about the only cup of coffee I have all day that I can enjoy from start to finish. Jonah is engrossed in his show so I go out onto my deck to enjoy my coffee and sneak a cigarette. The day is warm and the sun is shining bright already. I plop myself down onto my rocker and look out over the lake in my backyard. My mind isn't focused on too much other than what mundane chores to begin first. Laundry, dishes, vacuuming? The list is long but my thoughts are short with just one: John.

I'm thinking of his naked body entwined with mine. I'm thinking of each sweet kiss and the scent of him. I'm thinking of exploding into passion at the same exact moment with him.

I feel as though I'm caught in the middle of two worlds. One as a wife and mother and one as a lover and there are days I wonder how I'm doing both. I'm living a lie with my husband and a life of truth with John. There is no middle ground here. It simply is what it is.

And some days it's confusing.

Yet most days it's comforting.

I had a quick dinner with my family and headed upstairs to get ready to go out. I love going to Park Place and I know that the band playing tonight is a good one.

I searched through my closet for the perfect outfit, choosing a pair of tight jeans, an off the shoulder white shirt and my spiked heels. "Not too bad," I thought.

Next was makeup and hair. I went a little heavier on my makeup seeing that we'd be going out at night. John called that look my "war paint!" Still, it looked good and I felt good.

Before long I could hear John downstairs talking to my dad. I headed down to the living room and said, "All set, let's go! We're picking up Colleen and Frank."

"Got it, boss lady!" he joked back and with that we said goodbye to my dad and got into the car. Colleen lived only a few minutes away and Frank and she were waiting on the front porch for us. They jumped in the car and we were off.

John lit a joint and we passed it around to one another on the drive to Asbury Park. Frank had a couple of rum shooters in his pocket and gave one to each of us.

"Cheers!" we all said as we drank the whole shot down.

We hit the circuit in Asbury Park and John thought it'd be fun to do a few laps around it. The circuit was the place that my mom told me never to drive on.

"There's drag racing and drugs!" she'd say, but that never stopped me.

So here we were, driving around the Circuit, checking out all the other people in their cars. Some were drag racing and it seemed that everyone was smoking pot. "Hmmm, maybe my mom was right!" I laughed to myself.

We parked the car and headed into the bar. The door girl checked our ID, took our cover charge and we went in. The band was just warming up so we tried to get as close to the stage as we could.

Colleen and I found a spot and sent John and Frank for drinks. They came back with four rum and cokes. The four of us stood huddled near the stage, sipping our drinks while trying not to spill them as the crowd bumped into us.

The lights came on and the band began to play. I love Southern Rock and this band is awesome. We danced in our spots and sang out loud. We were having such a good time until John handed me his drink and said, "Hold this, be right back."

There was a red headed girl near the door looking directly at him. I watched him as he walked towards her. She leaned into him to whisper in his ear. I saw him reach into his pocket and pull out money. He looked around nervously and cautiously, placing the money in her front pocket then reaching his hand into her other pocket and taking something out.

"What the hell was he doing and who the hell is this girl?" I thought to myself. By this time Colleen had noticed what was going on and said to me, "Who is that?"

"I have no idea. He didn't tell me a thing except to hold his drink," I said angrily.

"He's buying coke," Frank said matter of factly.

"What? He's buying what?" I asked with a very angry tone.

"He didn't tell you?" Frank said. "He knows her from work and wanted to score some for tonight."

"Fuck that," I said. "I'm not touching that stuff!" I said.

"Me either," said Colleen.

Once John's little "transaction" was complete he walked back towards me, took his drink from my hand and gave me a kiss on the cheek.

"What the hell are you thinking?" I yelled. "Coke?"

"Relax, just wanted to try it. No big deal," he said ever so casually.

"John, don't do it. The weed is enough. Why do you need that? And, what was all the touching with that girl? You had to reach into her pockets?" I asked, demanding an explanation.

"Hey, calm down. I can do what I want, you know. You're not married to me yet," he yelled back. He was angry and annoyed but I didn't care.

"No, we're not married. We're not really engaged either because you won't tell our parents!" I yelled back.

"Stop, just stop. We're out for a good night and you're ruining it," he said. He was stoned, very stoned and I hated when he got like this.

Colleen pulled me to the side and said, "Listen, we saw some other friends here. We're going to leave with them. You handle your boyfriend,

fiance, whatever the hell he is. I'm not getting myself mixed up with drugs,"
she said angrily.

"I don't blame you. I'm so sorry," I apologized.

"Why? He's the ass, not you. He should have told you why we really
came here," she said.

"Can I go with you? I don't want to be around him like this. I don't
know what he'll be like when he does that stuff," I pleaded.

"Sure, let's get out of here," she said.

"I'm leaving with Colleen and Frank," I said to John. "I'm really pissed
that you bought that and I can't believe you're going to use it."

"Then leave. Suit yourself. I'm staying," he said. I wondered if he had
already done coke before tonight.

"Fine. See you," I said and with that I walked away with Colleen and
Frank.

I turned back to look at John and saw him with that red headed girl
again.

I have no idea what's happening but ever since the night we got engaged
things have changed.

My heart was really starting to hurt.

Chapter 14

John called me late at night to tell me that he had a business trip coming up in Miami and he wanted me there.

"John, how am I going to get away from the kids? Richie is already in a bad mood about me smoking, I can't imagine he'll be thrilled that I'm going to go away for a few days and FAR away," I said, sounding thrilled but a bit nervous.

"Babe, you can do it. Do it for me. Do it for us. It's just a few days. Tell him you're going on a girls getaway for the weekend with Colleen. It'll do him good to be by himself and it'll do you good to be with me," he said convincingly "You know that I'd go anywhere with you, it's just that this time it's for a few days, not just one night," I said hoping that he would understand just what I was putting on the line here.

"Listen, if you don't want to go, then don't. I'm going whether you go or not, but I would love it if you're with me. Warm weather, beautiful sunsets and passionate lovemaking every chance we get. But, if it's too much trouble…" he said, knowing exactly what I'd say back to him.

"Okay, I'll do what I can. I hope it's worth the risk that we're both taking," I said.

"Babe, WE'RE worth any risk. I love you," and once again he had me at "I love you."

I hated fighting with John. I could never win an argument. We didn't fight often but when we did, oh boy…

I was usually the one to give in because I didn't want to lose him.

"I don't know why you had to buy cocaine!" I yelled.

"I wanted to try it and if you want to know, I didn't like it," he said, almost chiding me into an argument with him.

"What about the girl? Did you sleep with her or just do drugs with her?" I asked and believe me, I wasn't asking nicely.

"Screw the girl. She had what I wanted, that's all. I did a line with her and spent the rest of the night feeling good and enjoying the band. What, I'm not allowed to do that?" he said sarcastically.

"Do whatever you want. I don't want you doing cocaine. I don't want you hanging out with that girl," I answered.

"Oh, I see, I can do whatever I want but I can't, have I got that straight?" he said to me ever so arrogantly.

"Why do you have to make everything so difficult?" I asked.

"Because you make it difficult!" he replied.

"Why is it always my fault? Why is it always me making things difficult?" I asked with a very annoyed tone.

"Because it always is. I was fine. No problems with me. Just you with the problems. You need to lighten up," he answered.

"Then I guess it's me," I said, not meaning one word of it.

"Okay, are we done arguing now?" he asked.

I wasn't sure if I loved him at this moment or hated him for always blaming me for everything. He was right, I was wrong, it was a pattern with us, yet I kept taking it and allowing it.

"Sure, we're done arguing," I answered, feeling defeated yet again.

"Good, give me a kiss and I'll make it all better," he said with a tone I didn't much care for.

He gave me a kiss on the lips, his tongue yet again finding mine.

"You know I love you," he said with an impish grin.

And once again, he had me at "I love you."

Chapter 15

"Would you mind if I went away for a weekend with Colleen? A little girl's trip to just catch up and have some fun," I said with my fingers crossed behind my back.

"Yeah, that's fine. You'll have a great time, I'm sure. Where are you going?" he asked as if he couldn't wait for me to leave.

"Miami," I answered.

"Are you flying or driving?" he asked because he knew about my fear of flying "I know, that's the only downfall, but I have to face my fears sometime and this is the perfect time," I said, trying to sound convincing. I was afraid of flying but more afraid of John being there alone and filling my spot in the bed with someone else.

"I'll have a few drinks before I get on the plane," I joked.

"Oh, I'm sure you will. And a few cigarettes too, right?" he responded.

I hate him.

"You didn't need to go there but sure, whatever you say is the truth," I responded with a snarky tone in my voice.

"Well, alright then. Book your flight and I'll get my comfy chair ready for me to work from home," he said, almost happily.

"Thanks, I really do appreciate you letting me go," I said thankfully, all the while meaning that I was thankful that he was letting me fly to Florida to sleep with his boss.

I went back to folding the laundry, all the while daydreaming of making hours of love to John. I was wet with excitement as I stood folding Richie's briefs. Wet with excitement at knowing that in two short weeks I'd be naked and one with John.

Life was moving along pretty damn good today.

Once again time marched on and it was graduation day. I couldn't believe that it was here already! Four long years of high school were about to end and we'd be moving onto the next chapter of our lives. I was nervous and excited at the same time.

My mom had decorated the house for her first born graduating from high school. She had balloons and flowers and even special ordered a cake done in red and blue, my school colors.

Colleen and I were on the phone at least once every hour trying to figure out what we were going to wear and what best way to do our hair so that our cap would fit just right.

My mom called for me from downstairs, "You want a little dinner before we go?"

"No, I'm not hungry," I said. I don't think dinner would have fit into my stomach with all the butterflies that had taken up residence.

"Well, you should try and eat something," she tried to persuade me.

My phone rang and it was John.

"This is it, babe, the day we've been waiting for. You ready?" he asked excitedly.

"I'm ready to graduate and trying hard not to think of us leaving each other in August.

"Don't even think about that tonight! Let's go graduate and party! I'll be at your house in a half hour to get you. Be ready," he said.

"Almost ready. See you soon," I said.

"Oh, and babe?" he asked.

"Yeah?" I answered.

"I love you," he said.

"Right back at 'ya," I said.

John was at my house in just under thirty minutes. My mom had pressed my gown and had it hanging on a hanger.

"Try not to get this wrinkled!" she ordered.

"I won't," I said and we headed out the door and into the car.

We got to the high school and walked into the gym where we put on our cap and gowns. Soon we took our places in the line up and proceeded onto the football field. I was so nervous but this was so cool!

After several speeches, it was time! As each graduates name was called over the loudspeaker we walked to the podium to receive our diploma. When the last name was called they announced "Class of 1979, You Have Graduated!"

We threw our caps into the air, hugging the people sitting close to us.

And just like that, we were graduates. High school was over and college was only a few short months away.

We all met with our family and friends to take pictures before we headed home.

John was going to pick me up in an hour to go to our graduation party at Pat's 30 Acres. There was going to be a live band and more kegs of beer than we could imagine.

The time passed by quickly and I was home, changed and ready to party and celebrate this night!

John came running through the door with such a smile on his face.

"We did it! No more high school!" he sang.

"Yes we did!" I said as I smiled back, walked over to him and gave him a hug and a kiss.

"Wow, you feel even better now that you're a college student!" I joked.

"Haha, very funny. You do, too, babe, now let's get out of here!" he said.

We said goodbye to my parents and told them not to wait up. Knowing our class we'd be partying until sunrise, or at least be hanging at the beach for it!

We drove to Pat's 30 Acres, parked the car and headed to the party. We had red solo cups of beer flowing all night. We danced, we drank and we smoked pot. Life was awesome right about now.

I tried to keep the thoughts of John and I being away from each other when we left for college, but they were there.

"Oh, fuck it," I said to myself. "Enjoy tonight and worry about the rest later."

And with that I did.

Chapter 16

The two weeks until Miami passed quickly. The kids had so many school activities during that time that I didn't have a moment to feel the anticipation of waiting for the days to pass.

And now the day is here.

My flight is scheduled for 6 pm tonight so I began my task of getting the house ready for my departure and myself ready for mine.

I made a few dinners for the family to eat while I was away. I must have done seven or more loads of laundry, a sure fire way of keeping my mind off of my upcoming flight tonight. I folded all of the clothes, putting each pile away as I did. This was not my usual method, I usually just left everything folded in their respective piles on the dining room table for each kid to grab to take to their room.

Not so now. I felt the need to leave the house as organized as I could, as if for the possibility that I might not come home. I didn't know if that was more out of my fear of the plane crashing or the hope that John would want me to stay forever. Nothing was making sense at the moment. I wanted to go but knew that I shouldn't. I wanted to spend the rest of my life with John but knew that he couldn't.

I wanted...I wanted...I wanted.

But I was used to a lifetime of never really having what I wanted. Why would it be any different now?

I shook my head as if that would stop all of these thoughts from racing through my mind. I went back to plugging away at the tasks at hand, cleaning the house, getting meals prepared and organizing life for the kids without me.

But all of these chores didn't prevent my mind from wandering to the reality of what I was really doing, or should I say, of what I was about to do.

The hours of the day passed by at lightning speed, thank God. Before I knew it, my oldest was coming through the front door from school. He came into the kitchen, gave me a hug, grabbed a snack and headed to his room. I heard his door shut and the sounds of "Stairway to Heaven" began resonating through the kitchen ceiling. Ah, to be young again!

An hour later my daughter came home, following the same pattern as her brother, although she spent a bit more time chatting with me, knowing that I was leaving soon.

Time marched on and I put a quick dinner of spaghetti and meatballs on the stove. I knew that I certainly wouldn't be eating any of it. My stomach was in knots, filled with guilt, filled with want. I went back upstairs to finish packing.

I carefully folded my lime green dress, a black and a white tank top, along with my sexy lingerie that I had bought just for John and put them into the suitcase. John had told me how sexy he thought I would look in a tank top, so I brought them. I knew that the temperature in Miami would be warm enough to wear them outside and I knew that the temperature in our hotel room would be warm enough not to wear anything at all.

I grabbed a pair of jeans, some khakis, and a couple of Gap t-shirts. I packed a pair of pajamas, knowing full well that they'd never be worn. John loved to sleep in the nude and demanded, well, not exactly demanded, but strongly persuaded me to do the same. I have to admit, I've never been a fan of sleeping naked but I'd do it for him. I'd do anything for him.

Okay then, my suitcase is packed with everything that I need, except for loyalty and trust. Let's face it, I wasn't really bringing those along. There wasn't enough room in my suitcase for them.

After all, an affair doesn't usually begin with loyalty and trust.

I lugged it down the stairs hoping that it wouldn't be deemed "overweight" at the airport. I grabbed my pocketbook, stuffed my tablet and book into it, and hid my cigarettes deep down in the outside pocket. I lined everything up at the front door and went back to the kitchen to fulfill my final role as a mother before I left to become an adultress.

Richie walked through the front door just as I was getting dinner on the table.

"Smells good. Spaghetti and meatballs, I'm guessing?" he said, dropping his computer at the front door along with his shoes.

"Good guess. Are you hungry?" I asked as I was calling the kids to the table. "Yeah, aren't you?" he asked, noticing that I hadn't set a place at the table for myself.

"Too nervous. My stomach feels a bit funny," I answered. I couldn't tell if it felt that way over flying or over John.

"You should try to eat something before you go. There won't be any food on your flight," he said with concern. I couldn't imagine why he was concerned now. That concern should have come 10 years ago when our marriage started to go downhill.

"I'll be fine. I'll grab a granola bar to take with me and if I feel up to it, I'll grab something to eat at the airport," I answered knowing that with this type of nervousness it would be a "liquid" dinner.

The four of them sat down at the table, scoffing down the spaghetti and garlic bread. I sat down with my family and listened to all the chatter that comes from my kids all talking at once. Richie chimed in here and there but the kids definitely had the floor.

I loved this time of day. My whole family would sit down to dinner together, just "us." This was the time of day that there was no annoying noise of the television or distractions from their cell phones. It's one of those rare moments as they get older that I get to see them all together, Richie included. The kids were rambling on endlessly tonight, an occasional "difference of opinion" cropping up between them, to which Richie and I always responded the same: "No arguing at the dinner table. No negative talk, only positive," if not just for this one meal, anyway. The bickering would end almost immediately to which Richie and I would flash each other a smile across the table, remembering what dinnertime was like when we were children.

This time when Richie smiled at me our eyes met for more than a second and he seemed to look right into my soul. I remembered what it was like when we first fell in love in college, just a year or two after John and I broke up. I held my smile back with his, realized how lucky I was to have these beautiful children, this wonderful home, and to have Richie.

My God, I'm having second thoughts.

"I have the perfect guy for you. His name is Richie. You guys would get along great. You both smoke and love to drink pot after pot of coffee!" my roommate, Michelle joked.

"Oh, and this is what a great relationship is made of? Cigarettes and caffeine?" I laughed.

"Just go out with him once. Okay? He told me that he thought you were cute, not to mention very sexy. Give the poor guy a chance," she pleaded.

"Oh fine. Set something up for this Friday night. I'm staying on campus this weekend anyway," I told her. I could hear her grabbing her cell phone and telling him what I said.

"He'll pick you up at six on Friday. He said to tell you to dress nice because he's taking you to a nice restaurant in Princeton for dinner," she said. Wow, he sounds a bit controlling already.

Great, I thought, what the hell am I going to wear? I was more of a jeans and t-shirt kind of girl and now I had to buy something new that I'd never wear again. Fuck that, I thought. I wasn't quite sure if Richie was worth spending my money on. I'll ask Leslie what she's got that I can borrow. There's actually some benefits of living with two female roommates!

Leslie was the fashion guru of our little tribe of girls and I was sure that she would know exactly what I should wear to fit in with an Ivy League school kind of restaurant.

"This is a dream come true for me to finally dress you up," she joked. *"Finally you'll be in something other than jeans."*

She rustled through her closet and found not one, but three outfits for me to try on. Ugh, I can't believe that I'm going through all of this for a *guy that I don't know. I was already NOT looking forward to this date and very much regretting that I had agreed to go at all.*

Friday night came and Leslie had managed to talk me into wearing her knee length tweed skies, tight with a split up the front, a silky button down white shirt, and knee high brown leather dress boots. I looked like an Ivy Leaguer myself! The doorbell rang promptly at six and I heard Michelle open the door.

"Hey, Richie, she's just about ready. Coffee?" she asked in a joking tone of voice. "No thanks, I'm good," he answered with a slight tone of annoyance towards her.

I walked out into the livingroom and there in front of me was Michelle with this sandy colored hair guy. Oh, God, I only date brunettes! First red flag! He was just shy of six feet tall, extremely thin, yet kind of cute in his own way. She introduced us and he shook my hand.

Seriously? Who shakes hands on a first date?

"Hi, it's nice to meet you. Ready to go?" he asked.

"Sure, I'm ready. Bye girls," I said to Michelle and Leslie.

And with that he opened the front door for me and led me to his car. It was a black Dodge Charger. Ok, this was cool. He opened the door for me and helped me in. He got in and we were off for our dinner in Princeton. We talked on the way to the restaurant, mostly about school and about how Michelle thought we were a great match. Small talk but at least "talk."

We pulled up in front of a very posh restaurant in Princeton, valet service and all. Not too shabby for two college kids! The valet extended his hand out to me to help me out of the car and Richie met me around the side, taking my hand in his. A little presumptuous, I thought, but truth be told, it felt kind of nice. He had made reservations for us and we were seated right away.

"Do you mind if I order for you?" he asked. I don't know, I thought to myself, this guy seems to like to be in control but since it was a first date I wanted to see just what he was made of.

"Sure, but no seafood. I don't like it much," I answered.

"No seafood it is. How about a glass of wine?" he asked.

"Sure, that would be great," I answered knowing damn well that I hated wine. I was a beer kind of girl myself, but this is Princeton and I

don't think ordering a beer in this restaurant would be taken well. In fact, I wouldn't be at all surprised if they didn't have beer!

The waiter came over to the table to tell us about the specials of the evening, then stepped back and waited for a response from Richie.

"The lady and I will have the chicken cordon bleu, salad with house dressing and to drink I'd like to order a bottle of your best white wine," Richie said, very sure of himself. He was starting to impress me with his ease and of how sure he was about himself. I wondered if he was that sure or just that arrogant?

"Very well, sir," the waiter said and was off to get the wine. He came back in a few minutes with a silver bucket that stood on a silver pedestal. I chuckled to myself and thought, "We're definitely not in Kansas anymore!"

He poured a small amount of wine into Richie's glass. He swirled it around, took a sniff of it and tasted it.

"This will be fine," he said. The waiter then filled my glass and replenished his. He walked away and told us that our salads would be out shortly.

"Here's to a nice evening," Richie said, holding his glass up to toast mine.

"To the evening," I responded, clinking my glass with his. We took a sip of our drinks and got our cigarettes out at the same time. He reached over to light mine for me. This guy sure knew all the right things to do to impress me. We smoked and talked and our conversation that had been nothing more than idle chit chat in the car was turning into one of a more personal nature. We started to really get to know each other. We continued to talk through bitefuls of salad and throughout our main course.

Richie ordered a wonderful desert of creme brulee for each of us and of course, coffee!

The dinner was almost over and I was starting to feel sad that it was going to end. I was really beginning to enjoy his company and dare I say, I was starting to like him, really like him in a way that I hadn't liked anyone since John.

Richie paid the check and we got back into the car. We continued to talk the entire drive back to my apartment. He walked me to the door. I was hoping for a nice, long kiss goodnight but instead he thanked me for a lovely evening and kissed me on the cheek.

And then he left.

I walked into my apartment, completely perplexed about this guy. He wasn't like anyone I had met before, yet he just did something to me that no one has since John…he made my heart feel something again.

Chapter 17

The stare that Richie and I were engaged in was abruptly broken with my son yelling, "Mom, the limo's here!"

Limo? I knew that Richie had arranged for a car to take me to the airport but I certainly wasn't expecting a limo! I jumped up out of my chair and looked out the window to find a black stretch limo parked in front of our house.

"Richie, what the hell did you do? You didn't need to get me a stretch!" I said to him with excitement in my voice, all the while secretly feeling glad that he had gotten it for me.

"You deserve it. The last time you were in a limousine was for our wedding. I think it's time that you had another ride in one. Enjoy yourself. You deserve this trip and some time away with your friend," he said as he walked up to me at the front door, slipping his arm around my shoulder and kissing the side of my head.

Just when I think I know Richie he does something wonderful. It's been like that our entire marriage. When I think I'm safe in not feeling anything for him he does something that makes me feel good again.

And I hate that. It feels as though he's playing a game with me, except I'm not playing yet losing at the same time. Right now I couldn't worry about it or even utter a thought of care about it.

The kids were outside by now and in the limo, playing with the radio and television. I'm sure that the driver was relieved when he saw me come out with just one suitcase!

"Okay, you two, out you go. I have to get to the airport. Give me a hug and kiss and go back into the house with your dad," I said, handing my bag to the driver and strongly encouraging the kids to get out of the car.

"No fair, we never get to drive in a limo!" they yelled in protest.

"Let's go, guys, Mom doesn't want to miss her flight," Richie said to them. He grabbed my little guy out of the car and handed him to me. He wrapped his little arms around my neck, slobbering his kisses all over my face, to which I covered his face with mine, all the while committing his smell of innocence to my memory. I was beginning to feel an ache in my heart at leaving my three kids and of leaving Richie.

Maybe this whole thing wasn't such a good idea. I stopped my mind from racing by thinking "No, I have to go." I told myself that I'd think about things on the plane and make a decision about what to do by the time I get to Miami.

My little one was beginning to squirm in my arms so I gave him one last big squeeze and a big "I'm stuck on you" kiss. I put him down and watched him run around in circles on the front lawn.

"C'mon, guys, Mom has to go. One last goodbye," Richie yelled to the kids. They ran up to me and through the kisses and hugs I reminded each one of them just how much I love them. They ran off and went back to what they were doing.

"I'll see you in a few days. Relax, the flight will be fine and you'll be fine, too. I'll take good care of the kids. Go and have a good time," and with that Richie hugged me in a way that he hadn't in years and planted a big, wet kiss on my lips. I wondered if he had a small suspicion of what was going on or if he was beginning to be fearful of his wife's "new found freedom." In any event, I had to make this trip one way or another.

I have a decision to make about John.

And I only have a two hour flight to do it in.

"Bye, Richie. Thanks again for letting me go," I said half heartedly, wishing now that he hadn't let me go.

"I love you," he said and I couldn't remember the last time he said that to me. "Love you, too," I answered back, wondering if I really meant it.

"It'll be late when you land so shoot me a text that you got there okay and call me in the morning?" he said.

"Sure, see 'ya," I said.

And with that I got into the limo, closed the door and waved goodbye. I watched out of the car window until it got to the end of the street. I could see the kids as they played Frisbee on the front lawn and watched as Richie swept our youngest up into his arms and kissed him.

I watched my family and wondered what in the world possessed me into taking such a risk and losing all of this?

Richie wined and dined me every day for a week after our dinner in Princeton, all the while charming and impressing me more each time we were together. He'd pick me up from work and have a long stemmed rose waiting for me on the seat of the car. He'd bring me a bottle of Bailey's Irish Cream to share with me poured over some Hagen Daz vanilla ice cream.

And yet, in all this time, he never kissed me on the lips, just on my forehead. I couldn't get over what a gentleman he was! What college guy is like that? Most would have taken you to bed by now!

He picked me up from work one afternoon during a very bad snowstorm. I remember he was wearing tight jeans and a white fishermans sweater. He told me that he didn't want me driving in such bad weather, afraid that I might have an accident. I got into the car, a big bouquet of carnations, my favorites, waiting for me on the seat.

"Richie! What did you do? They're beautiful!" I said, kissing him gently on the cheek.

"So are you," he said back. We didn't speak much on the ride back to my apartment, partially because he was concentrating on driving in a snow storm that was quickly turning into a blizzard.

And partially because he seemed genuinely nervous about something.

He held my hand on the drive back, barely looking at me. I wondered why, wondered if something was wrong but assumed he was just busy looking at the road. It took us twice the amount of time as usual to get to my apartment but I knew that was from the driving conditions. He pulled into my apartment complex and parked. We walked hand in hand until we got to the front door. He took my keys from me and unlocked the door, pushing it open for me to walk through first. We took off our coats and I went into the kitchen to make some coffee. "Where is everyone?" he asked me.

"Michelle is home for the weekend and Leslie is on some retreat. The place is all mine until Sunday night," I yelled from the kitchen.

I started the coffee maker and slid down on the couch next to Richie, snuggling up against him to grab some of his warmth. He slid his arm around me then used his other hand to guide my face to look up towards his. He brought his mouth down to meet mine and kissed me for the very first time. It was a long, soft kiss and he gently slid his tongue into my mouth cautiously, as if to see if I would reciprocate. I let his tongue meet mine and slid my arms around him. He pulled me up onto his lap to face him and began kissing me more passionately. I could tell from where I was sitting that he wanted me and I knew that I would let him have me. He picked me up, my legs wrapped around his waist, still kissing me as he fumbled down the hallway to my room

When he got to my door I reached over to turn the handle and push it open. He laid me down on the bed and began undressing me. I lay there naked as I watched him take his clothes off.

He was so thin that you could almost see his bones. He was so unlike John but just as appealing at this moment. He straddled my body and began to run his hands all over me. He cupped my breasts with his hand and began to fondle them until my nipples were hard. Then he put his mouth over them to excite them even more. I could already feel myself getting wet.

He slid down to the edge of the bed, moved my legs apart and began kissing me on my thighs. I could feel myself getting excited as his tongue worked its magic and its way all around and over me. Just as I was about to lose control he moved up and inside of me, thrusting harder and harder. It didn't take long before he lost all control of himself and when he rolled off of me I could feel the wetness of both of us on my legs. He laid down next to me and took me into his arms. I didn't know what to think of all of this. For the last few weeks he'd done nothing more than kiss me on the forehead.

And now he had just made love to me.

"I love you," he said and for a minute or so I had no response back to him. This seemed so sudden and I needed to think about saying it back but instead I turned to him and said, "I love you, too."

We fell asleep to the sounds of the icy snow pounding against the windows and for the first time since John I felt something that I hadn't since him...

I felt safe.

Chapter 18

I could feel my eyes welling up with tears as the limo pulled out of my street. I felt a wave of sadness at leaving my family and a bit angry at John for asking me to do this. It seems like the only times I could be with him were on his random business trips and it was beginning to feel that he only wanted me when it was convenient for him. He didn't have to make up a lie to his family to see me, yet I did. Guilt was beginning to consume every ounce of my being along with a resentment towards John that I hadn't felt until now. I didn't like feeling this way but I couldn't seem to shake it.

I kept thinking to myself "What is it with you and men? You're always with the controlling ones that call the shots and you go willingly."

Enough with that. I just couldn't go there right now. I was consumed by so many emotions that I felt like opening the door of the limo and jumping out. What the hell was I doing and WHY was I doing it? My God, I need to find some sense of balance, of peace with all of this. How did my life end up here?

All I could do at this very moment was pull out my tablet, a gift from Richie the night before. He had loaded Spotify on it with all of my favorite music. I just needed to figure out how to use it. I put on my headphones, figured out how to get into the app and within moments I was listening to Sheryl Crow.

"I wanna soak up the sun, wanna tell everyone to lighten up..." played through my headset, the tension in my body slowly melting away. My mind kept replaying the picture of Richie and the kids on the front lawn. I missed them so much already and my heart ached to be with them. I only hoped that John had some idea of the sacrifices that I made for him. If he didn't then I'd be damn sure that he would know by the end of tonight.

Could I possibly be hating the man I profess to love? Could I possibly be loving the man I profess to hate?

I let out a long sigh, closed my eyes and said a prayer to God to help me do the right thing.

But what was the right thing?

I wanted to be happy but my happiness would hurt so many.

And what's so good about that?

Next song, please.

The drive to the airport took little more than an hour and before I knew it the driver was helping me out of the car and handing me my suitcase.

"Don't I need to pay you?" I asked, definitely sounding like a fish out of water or at least a "mom out of water."

"No, ma'am, your husband took care of everything. He's a great guy! I'll be back to pick you up in a few days. Enjoy your trip with your girlfriend," he said as he got back into the limo and drove off.

Thanks, now I really feel like shit.

Great guy? Who, Richie?

Only when he wants to be.

And only when he wants to impress others.

And only when he wants to make me look like nothing.

So there I was, standing alone with my bag outside of the Delta door. I went in and found the e-ticket booth. A lovely older woman helped me through the process of getting my ticket and then pointed me in the right direction of my terminal.

"You look a little stressed, honey, don't be. Everything will be fine," she said as I grabbed my bag.

Lady, I thought to myself, you have no idea just how stressed I am.

And I was hoping that she was right because at the moment I'm not sure that anything will be fine.

My flight wasn't scheduled for departure for another hour so I bought a bottle of water and some chips and settled into a seat near the door. A young man sat down near me and we struck up a conversation. I told him how nervous I was about flying on such a small plane to which he calmed my fears by telling me that he flew this type of plane often and found it much more relaxing than a bigger plane. He was either a really good liar or was being truthful because I was beginning to feel a bit less nervous after chatting with him.

Still, there was enough time to hit the airport bar and grab a glass of wine or two.

I knew that there wasn't enough wine to calm these nerves or still this mind that just wouldn't turn off.

Before long the loudspeaker called for passengers to board the plane. I found my seat by the window and sat down, feeling grateful that no one would be sitting next to me.

There were so few people on this flight that everyone was sitting alone, unless they were a family.

Where were all these "single" people going and why?

There was a young couple a few rows ahead of me with a baby that looked to be a month old and a toddler who looked to be about the age of my youngest. I began to remember what it was like when Richie and I had just two little ones and in seconds I could feel my eyes welling up with tears over leaving my children and my husband.

Husband.

Now there's a word I hadn't used in my vocabulary in quite some time.

Why now?

I put my Airpods into my ear, turned on my tablet and stared out of the window.

The plane took off and we were high in a sky filled with vibrant orange and pink colors. I felt as though I was in the middle of the sunset, grateful to be a part of it. I had never felt so close to God and couldn't help but think to myself that this might be a good time to have a chat with Him about what I was doing. I prayed for Him to help me do the right thing and to make it easy to do.

None of this was going to be easy, not the staying and not the leaving.

I turned off the music and let myself go deep into thought. After thinking for most of the flight I knew what it was that I had to do. I had to break things off with John. I knew it would hurt us both and that we'd be broken hearted but I knew it was the right thing to do. We were both married with children. Neither of us had ever wanted to hurt our spouses yet by having this affair we were doing just that. They just didn't know that we were.

A wave of peace came over me in knowing that me breaking things off would be the right decision for us both. We could still enjoy our trip together but it would be our LAST trip. This affair needed to end and we needed to end it now before it went much further.

Lord knows it's already gone far enough.

A voice boomed over the loudspeaker of the plane announcing our impending landing. I took out my Airpods and tucked them and my tablet back into my bag. I buckled my seatbelt and stared out of the window as the sights below that had once been speckles of light were now becoming bigger. The plane slowly got lower and lower until I finally felt a few small bumps letting me know that we had landed and were safely on the ground.

I knew that I had to get off of the plane to meet John, who would be waiting for me in the airport to take me to the hotel. Our hotel. I also knew that instead of making love to him tonight as we had planned I was going to be following my plans to end our affair.

I got my luggage and headed to the nearest bathroom to freshen up my makeup, which I'm sure was "tear" stained from my emotions during the flight, and to brush my teeth. No matter what, I still wanted to look good when he saw me.

My cell phone rang and it was John.

"Hey, babe, where are you? I see that the plane landed and I'm waiting for you," he said with an excitement in his voice that made me feel a bit uneasy.

"Hey, I just made a pitstop in the bathroom. I'll see you in a minute or two," I answered. I was starting to feel something strange but I couldn't quite put my finger on it. Oh my God, what the hell is going on with me? Help me, please!

"I'll be waiting by the escalator. Hurry up, babe!" he yelled as he hung up his phone.

I finished touching up my makeup, quickly brushed my teeth and sprayed a bit of perfume on. I grabbed my bag and headed toward the escalator, which I could see ahead in the distance.

A few more steps and I was at the bottom of the escalator. Just as I was about to step on it I looked up and saw John standing there, a smile on his face which stretched from ear to ear. He saw me right away and raised his arm up to wave to me. I lifted my arm back and smiled up to him.

I was frozen and passengers were going around me to get on the escalator. It was as though my feet were stuck to the ground. This was the moment. This was the defining moment of "us."

Would I go to him or go away from him?

My heart skipped a beat as I saw him waiting for me. My eyes were fixed on him and his eyes on my entire ride up the escalator. It only took a few seconds to reach him but it felt like hours.

I reached the top and stepped off to the side where John was standing. He grabbed me into his arms in a giant bear hug and I grabbed him back, inhaling that familiar, beautiful smell of cigarettes and his cologne. He pulled back a bit then grabbed me tight into a long, passionate kiss which I gave right back to him.

He grabbed my hand in his and took my suitcase in his other hand as he led me out to his rental car.

It took less than five minutes to realize something that would change my life forever…

I love him and I will never, ever leave him.

It's been almost two weeks since Richie and I had made love for the first and only time. I hadn't seen him much and his phone calls were becoming less and less frequent. In fact, it's been three days since I've heard from him at all. I called and left voicemails but never heard back from him. My heart was starting to hurt and I had a sinking feeling of something bad happening.

What happened? We made love, he told me that he loved me and he spent the night. What could have possibly happened in two weeks?

And then one day he shows up out of the blue at my apartment door. No flowers, no Baileys, no kiss on the forehead, let alone the lips. There stood Richie, looking distant and cold, looking like a guy that was about to hurt me and looking like a liar.

"Hey you, I was beginning to think that you forgot about me," I chided, becoming acutely aware that something was definitely wrong. He looked at me as though I had meant nothing to him.

I stepped forward to give him a kiss but he immediately stepped back. What the hell is going on?

"Richie, what's wrong?" I asked KNOWING that something was wrong. I was so afraid of getting hurt and, judging by the way my stomach felt, I knew that I was about to.

"I can't see you anymore. I met someone else and I love her. I don't love you anymore," he said coldly.

"What? What the hell is that? You just told me you loved me TWO WEEKS ago and now you tell me that you don't and that you love someone else? What's that about? Are you sleeping with her? And how did you let that happen?" I asked, the anger in my voice shadowing the fear.

"It's just the way it is. And yes, if you need to know, I did make love to her and we're better together at it than you and I were that ONE time," he said, emphasis on the ONE time.

"I'm sorry, what can I say? I love her, I don't love you," he said matter of factly, so cool yet so cruel that I could have slapped him. How dare he make me feel worthless, like I never mattered at all. Who the hell was this girl that changed his mind about me in two weeks?

"She moved in with my roommates and I two weeks ago and we hooked up. And I love her," he said with a "this is the end of story" attitude.

"Oh, really? I didn't know that's how love worked. Thanks for clearing it up for me. Thanks for making me feel stupid. You bastard," I yelled and with that I gave into my instinct and slapped him across the face. "Get the hell out of here and don't ever come back. Go fuck yourself. I hope you'll both be happy!"

And with that he left, off to be with the "one" that he loved. The one that he loved this week. It was just two weeks ago that I was "the one" that he loved.

It's happening all over again.

I'm alone.

And I'm afraid.

Chapter 19

We hopped into the rental car and were on our way. John never stopped smiling, not for one minute. We each lit a cigarette, relaxed and began to talk on our drive to the hotel

"The hotel's not far from here. We'll be there in just a few minutes," he said, pausing for just a moment before he turned towards me, looked me in the eyes and said "God, I can't believe that you're really here. And you're all mine for the next three days! I just can't believe it, babe!" He kissed the top of my hand which he had been holding the entire time of the drive since we left the airport.

"Believe it, babe, I'm all yours," I answered back, the smile on my face just as big as the one on his.

It's funny that it was only a short while ago that I was thinking of ending things. Now it was the furthest thing from my mind. The closest thing to my mind at the moment was that I was completely focused on John, my John, my one and only John.

My one and only true love.

Now what?

I saw the hotel looming in front of us, or maybe it was gazing in front of us. It was surrounded by palm trees and brightly colored flowers. There was a large water fountain in the front with wind chimes surrounding it. It felt like nirvana.

John pulled into the parking lot and we got out of the car. He grabbed my suitcase and we walked in, hand in hand. We must have looked like a couple of newlyweds, excited with anticipation at the thought of knowing what we were going to be doing in a while. My body was nervously excited knowing what was to come and to literally "come." He's the one.

The only one.

The one who had been the only one since I first met him.

We got to the front desk and John and the girl behind it started chuckling, as she had just checked him in only an hour or so before. It's as if she already knew what we were doing, or at least, about to do. Who could blame her? I was thinking the same thing.

She welcomed me to the hotel, gave me my key and we were ready to go.

"I'm sure that you know how to get to her room, sir," she said, smiling at John as if she already knew the secret that we shared.

And I know that she did.

And so did I.

John looked at her and smiled, "Yeah, I know how to get her there!" And with that he took my hand in his and led me to the elevator.

We got to my room and John took my key from me and opened the door, letting me go through the door first. I immediately plopped myself down onto the bed, tired from the flight but not too tired from the evening that was about to happen.

John sat down by my feet and asked if I'd like a foot massage. He read my mind. He always could. I felt as though I had just entered heaven.

"You read my mind, babe. Rub away. I'm in need, for sure!" I answered back. And he did just that. He took out some lavender scented lotion that he had brought with him and slid off my shoes and socks. Lord knows that I needed some "calm" right about now.

He gazed into my eyes even while he put the lotion in his hands. He always believed that "the eyes were the windows to the soul" and knew that with me it was true. There's something incredibly erotic about a man staring into your eyes, filling his hands with lotion and rubbing your feet, all the while never taking his eyes off of you.

I was already excited.

And relaxed.

And ready.

We chatted for a bit about our flights and talked about the kids. We didn't mention a word about our spouses and for good reason.

I didn't want to think about Tess and he didn't want to think about Richie. "Babe, want to join me for a shower?" he asked with that seductive tone of voice and look on his face. He stared deep into my eyes, hoping I'd say "yes."

But I didn't.

"No, not really. I'd rather take a long, hot bath," I answered with my own seductive tone of voice.

"I really need a shower, babe. Won't you reconsider?" he pleaded.

"I'll tell you what, my love," I said, "you take a shower and when you're done, fill the tub and give me a shout when it's filled. I'd be happy to join you then." I thought it was a fair compromise and a clear statement that he's not going to get EVERYTHING he wants from me, even though it was pretty damn close that he did.

"Perfect," he said. "I'll give you a yell when I'm ready for you."

Nice one, John, you get "ready" because I'm definitely "ready" for you!

He left the door open as he showered and after about ten minutes or so I heard the noise of the water from the showerhead change to the sound of the water running from the faucet.

Damn, he really was going to fill a bath for me!

"Ready!" he yelled from the bathroom. I got up off of the bed and walked in through the door to see him, naked, sitting in the bathtub, waiting for me.

I knew that he loved visuals so I took my time and undressed slowly, allowing him a full view of every piece of clothing that I took off. I slid into the tub to sit in front of him, my back pressed into his chest.

He wrapped his arms around me and pulled me close.

"I can promise you that this will be a bath to remember," he said as he soaped up his hands. I can't even begin to tell you how and what I was feeling. He was my everything and was about to do everything to me.

He slid his soapy hands down my arms, to my fingers, then back up to my shoulders. It felt so incredibly good. I closed my eyes in anticipation of what I most assuredly knew was to come.

I sunk down a little lower into the tub, his hands searching for my breasts and once he found them, he began caressing them.

He traveled down towards my stomach, rubbing it in small circles. Next thing I knew, his hands were rubbing the top of my thighs, then my inner thighs, finally caressing me in the spot that I wanted him to be inside of.

I leaned back into his shoulder with a sigh that could stop a heart.

"John, take me to bed," I said as he kissed me long and hard. Long and hard. Hard and long.

We got out of the tub, dried off a big and hit the bed, where we were both lying facing one another. We began kissing and touching one another, knowing the exact spot that turned each of us on.

And we surely did touch!

John's hands were all over my body, probing deep inside of me, making me squirm with each movement, each twitch of his fingers.

"Make love to me," I whispered into his ear.

And he heard exactly what I said.

He rolled over on top of me and entered slowly, not thrusting deep inside, but gliding himself gently deeper and deeper into me until he was touching me in the exact place that no man has ever been able to touch me. He made love to me slowly, all the while staring into my eyes. At one point he told me to watch him as he made love to me and I knew what he had meant. We had "watched" ourselves make love to each other many, many years ago, just like tonight. Together we gazed down to watch as he slid himself into me, out of me, and then back in. Our gaze was fixed upon the love happening between us and he looked up at me and kissed me hard, our tongues making a love all of its own.

I let my hands travel down the curves of his back, grabbing his bottom and caressing him, sliding my hands back up to his shoulders. I took his sweet face into my hands, feeling his face, his cheeks, and the back of his neck. I took it all in and let my heart take a picture. I traced his lips with my index finger before showering him with soft kisses on his top lip, and then on his bottom.

He began kissing my neck and I closed my eyes.

I let my head sink backwards and allowed myself the pleasure of knowing how wonderful it felt to have him inside of me.

John grabbed my leg and rolled me over, wrapping his arms around me and entering me from behind, gently caressing my nipples which were hard with excitement. Our movements became quicker, our breather faster. I could feel my love for him building up deep inside of me and I knew that the moment we were striving for was near.

"Come with me, babe. Come with me," he said in a whisper and that was all it took. Within seconds we were at our peak together, all of me exploding onto him and all of him exploding into me. He stayed inside of me as we sunk down onto the bed, our bodies glistening in sweat.

And covered in the essence of each other.

I don't know if we fell asleep or just lost track of time before I realized that John's head was buried in my hair. He said, "I love you so much. This is where we're supposed to be."

And with that he gently slid himself out from within me and took up residence on my chest. I caressed the top of his head with my fingertips and listened to his heavy, rapid breathing become slower, calmer.

I glanced over at the clock to see that it was almost three in the morning. I couldn't even believe that we had been making love for almost four hours.

And this was just the beginning.

We had two more nights together.

We fell into a deep sleep together in each other's arms, ready to dream of a life together...

Of a life together that we both knew would never come to pass...

I hadn't seen Richie in months when we bumped into each other at a party.

"Hey there, stranger," he said as he lightly touched my shoulder. I moved it back away from his hand.

"Hey yourself," I answered, taking a long gulp of my beer.

"Whatcha been up to?" he asked and I thought to myself "Like you care."

"Not much, just hanging out," I said, looking around in the hopes that a familiar face would come over and rescue me from him.

"Sounds like a plan, and hey, about what happened between us…" he started to say before I could cut him off abruptly.

"Water under the bridge, Richie, don't sweat it," I answered curtly.

"No, it's not. I felt really bad about it. Think we could at least be friends?" he asked, sounding pretty sincere.

"Sure, whatever. Give me a call sometime, okay? And I won't hold my breath. I gotta go. See 'ya around," I answered and with that I left the party.

He'll never call, I thought.

But I was wrong.

True to his word he did call and I was sure to give him every sorted detail of every guy that I had gone out with since he left me. I held nothing back, which is what probably brought him back to me. I wondered if it was that old saying of "I don't want you but I don't want anyone else to want you either."

In time I'd learn that this is who Richie really is.

He showed up at my parents house one summer afternoon. I was getting ready to go out when I saw him. His car was blocking mine in the driveway and to say I was surprised was an understatement.

"Hey, what the hell are you doin', blocking my car in?" I joked with him.

"Trying to keep you home!" he joked back. He came up to me and we started talking, which led to driving to Bar Anticipation to grab a drink together. The drink turned into dinner and an offer to go to Atlantic City for the weekend.

"Sure, I'll go, but only as friends. That's the deal and I mean it," I said to him.

"Whatever you say, lady, you're the boss!" he answered, although I knew him well enough to know that he was just saying what he knew I wanted to hear. "Is next weekend good for you?" he asked.

"Next weekend is fine, but let's not leave too late in the day. Summer traffic on the parkway is a bitch on Fridays. Where are we staying?" I asked.

"My boss has a house there that he's gonna let us use for the weekend. Separate bedrooms, just as I'm sure you'd want it, unless..." he said laughing.

"You got that right. Separate bedrooms for sure. See you next weekend," I said, and with that he dropped me back at my parents house.

Chapter 20

It was about six in the morning when I first opened my eyes. It wasn't the morning light peeking through a small opening in the curtains that woke me, but instead it was John's snoring! I rolled to my side to look over at him. I watched him as he slept, his chest rising and falling with each breath. I touched his lip and watched him swat it with his hand as if a bug had landed on him. It made me smile.

His snoring continued but surprisingly enough it was like music to my ears. His eyes twitched a bit as he slept, making me wish that I could somehow get inside of his head to see what he was dreaming about. My eyes moved down along the outline of his body under the sheets and I could tell by the rise under them just what it was he might be dreaming about.

I slid my hand down under the sheet, placing it around the erection that he had apparently gotten while he was asleep. I began to run my hands up and down, watching his face to see if this might wake him up.

I was right.

He woke up.

He started to open his eyes and had that quirky smile on his face knowing what he was about to get. I removed my hand from him, kissed his lips and slid down under the sheets, enticing him further with my mouth. His hands reached for my long, dark hair which he began to run his fingers through. I savored the taste of him and continued with the task at hand (no pun intended!) until I felt ready to have him inside of me.

I slid up from under the sheet, climbed on top of him and straddled him, taking all of him deep inside of me. I heard him moan softly and knew that he was quite pleased with his morning "wake up" call.

I continued my up and down motion on top of him, swirling my hips now and again, much to his pleasure. He was wide awake now and took my arms into his hands, rolling me off of him until I was underneath him, all the while staying inside of me.

He pleasured me in ways that were unimaginable to me until just now. I whispered to him, just as he did to me on the night before, "Come with me."

He obeyed with immense pleasure and groaned with sounds that literally came from deep within him. I followed suit with the sounds of a woman reaching her ultimate peak of excitement. He rolled off of me more quickly than the night before and this time it was my head that rested on his chest.

"Good morning, love. This was the time that you wanted your wake up call, wasn't it?" I joked with him.

"Very funny. Do this to me every morning and I just may have to pack you in my bag to take you home with me," he joked back. Oh, how I wish he could!

I don't remember how long we laid like that but I must have fallen asleep because the next thing I remember was waking up to the smell of fresh coffee. John had quietly gotten out of bed, taking his time not to disturb me and wake me up. He ordered room service and waited in the hallway to get it, once again being mindful not to wake me.

Room service arrived with a large pot of coffee and a basket of pastries and bagels.

I opened my eyes to see a steaming cup of coffee on the nightstand next to me. I sat up and took a sip. He made it just the way I like it.

"He remembered," I thought to myself. He knew all the right things to do, right down to how I like my coffee.

"I have to take a shower and get ready for my appointments," he said with a trace of disappointment in his voice. "After all, this IS a business trip."

"I know, I know," I said, a disappointed tone in my own voice. "I decided to rent a car today and go sightseeing!"

"Good for you. I hate the thought of you locked up in this room all day just waiting for me to come home," he said. Home, he said, I wish this was "our home."

"Go and take your shower, babe. I'm going to have another cup of coffee and get my day started," I said, slipping out from underneath the sheets. He watched as my naked body walked over to him to grab him under his bathrobe, pressing myself hard against him.

"Hey, don't get me going again, I have to work. The sooner I get going, the sooner I get back home to you," he laughed, lovingly pushing me away as he headed for the shower.

"Ohhhh, alright," I said, pretending to sound really disappointed. We smiled at one another as he closed the bathroom door and I walked over to grab another cup of coffee and a pastry.

There I sat in my hotel bathrobe in the comfy chair by the window. I had opened the curtains to let the brilliant sunshine come in. I had my feet up on the ottoman, coffee in one hand, a delicious cheese danish in the other watching the local news on television.

Before long the bathroom door opened and out he came. He was dressed in a black two piece suit with a crisp, white dress shirt and red tie. He looked gorgeous, even handsome, and my heart melted at the sight of him.

He joined me for a cup of coffee and a quick bite of my pastry for himself.

"Sorry, babe, gotta run! That wake up call made me run a bit behind schedule," he joked, all the while smiling at me.

"I'll see you around four or so, hopefully earlier if I can wrap things up. In any case, I already have dinner plans for us so don't eat without me," he said as if he were giving me an order.

"Aye, aye, sir!" I joked with him.

I got up to walk over and give him a kiss goodbye. He had a small crumb of my pastry on his lip, which I kissed off of his mouth.

"You're funny. Give me a kiss goodbye that will hold me throughout the day and I'll see YOU tonight!" he said as he pulled me close to him and gave me a long, sensual kiss goodbye.

"I love you. Take that with you today," he said.

"I love you, too, John and you take that back with you," I said, blowing him a kiss as he walked towards the door.

I met him at the door, gave his bottom a little pat and told him to have a good day. He smiled, gave me a quick kiss on my lips and was gone.

I poured myself another cup of coffee and sat back down to watch a bit more television.

I had to prepare myself to call home, a task that would take a bit of work on my part. Lying didn't come easily to me and what I needed to do now was pretty simple...

I had to lie through my teeth.

It was Friday and Richie and his friend, Ted, were at my front door by four o'clock.

"I thought we were supposed to leave earlier, Richie! We're gonna hit so much damn traffic! What happened?" I asked with annoyance in my voice at leaving so late and his friend being with him.

"Shhhh, I had to wait for Ted. His wife and kids are there already and he needed a ride. I had to wait for him while he packed. It'll be fine. We're not in a hurry, are we? Maybe you're just dying to have your way with me!" he joked. I didn't think any of it was funny.

"No, you're wrong. I am definitely NOT dying to have my way with you, but I guess you're right, we're not in a hurry," I conceded. He always got the last word and always made sure he was right.

I grabbed my bag and said goodbye to my parents who were outside talking to Ted.

"See 'ya," I said to them, "I'll be back on Sunday, unless of course Richie kidnaps me or something!"

They waved goodbye and told us to be careful but to have a good time. Ted got into the backseat so that I could sit up front with Richie.

"Man, Richie, you have balls to just take her off for a weekend with her parents standing there! I can only imagine what her Dad was thinking!

Man, you have balls!" Ted said to him with somewhat of an envious tone to his voice, wishing that he had that kind of nerve.

"Shit, I didn't even think of that," Richie laughed. "Thank God your dad doesn't own a gun!" he paused for a moment, "does he?"

"No, he doesn't and you do have quite the set of balls!" I joked back with him.

We hit the Garden State Parkway within five minutes and within twenty we were in bumper to bumper traffic. Damn, this is gonna be a long drive, I thought to myself. There's nothing worse than Jersey Shore Summer traffic.

It actually turned out to be a pretty enjoyable ride as the three of us talked and laughed. We cracked open a few beers on the way and enjoyed the hot, sultry summer evening that was fast approaching. The windows were down, the radio playing and the balmy, hot summer breeze was blowing through our hair.

I had never met Ted before and this was the perfect time to get to know him, especially since Richie and he were good friends and co-workers. He talked about his wife and kids and how happy he was.

It took us almost five hours to get to Atlantic City but all in all, we made the best of it and actually had fun. Richie and I were a bit buzzed by the time we drove off the exit of the parkway, but not Ted. He knew his wife wouldn't take too kindly to him showing up drunk, especially since we were dropping him at his in-laws house!

We dropped him off and were on our way to his boss's house, or so I had thought.

"Yeah, about my boss's house," Richie said hesitantly, "Well, he rented it at the last minute so I got us a hotel room. Two beds, though," he added quickly.

"Are you kidding me? Why didn't you tell me that before we left? Geez," I said, trying to act mad even though I wasn't. Annoyed, maybe, but not mad.

I was actually looking forward to a weekend at the beach. Getting a tan and relaxing was just what I needed, even if it was a hotel with two beds.

"I'm sorry, really, I am," he said. I was beginning to think that Richie was a really good liar and that I was a really good pushover.

We pulled into the Breakers Hotel, just a block from the beach. Richie went into the office and got us registered. We parked the car, grabbed our bags and walked to our room. When he opened the door it didn't surprise me to see that there weren't two beds but one giant king size bed.

"Oh, sure," I thought, "like this wasn't his plan all along."

"Okay, okay, I know what you're thinking but I swear that this wasn't planned! The guy in the office just told me that since we were late checking in that this is all he had left, but if you want, I'll sleep on the floor or something, okay?" he said, his eyes staring up at me with a sad, puppy dog kind of look.

"Don't worry about it. It's fine. We can sleep in the same bed but not really sleeping together, okay? Don't get any ideas and I mean it," I said as firmly as I could.

"Okay, boss lady, whatever you say," he said. I could already tell by the look on his face that he had other plans, and as I've gotten to know him I've come to realize that he always gets what he wants, no matter what I want.

"Let's go grab some dinner and head out for some fun!" he said.

"It's a plan," I answered as I grabbed my turquoise mini dress from my suitcase. I headed into the bathroom to change, put on more makeup, spritzed myself with perfume and completed my ensemble with a pair of two and a half inch spike heels.

I walked back into the room and could tell in an instant from the look on his face that he was pleased.

Among other things.

"Nice," he said, smiling at me, "very nice."

"Thanks, Richie," I said, my heart softening a bit towards him. After all, he was paying for this entire weekend and God knows that I needed a break from work and from my parents.

We jumped back into the car and headed to the Lobster Shack. I couldn't help but think that Richie knew from our very first date in Princeton that I didn't like seafood. Seems that he forgot or as always, did what HE wanted to do.

We were seated at our table and ordered a beer. Richie didn't ask to order for me this time and I was fine with that. He ordered a lobster dinner and I opted for a NY strip steak with a baked potato. Judging by the look *on the waiter's face I don't think many people who come here do so for the steak! All in all, dinner was good and once he paid the check we decided to head down the road to a bar called "The Loop."*

The bar was crowded when we got there but there was a great band playing the perfect dance music, and dance we did. Richie was a pretty good dancer and I was having a great time.

I was also beginning to have those same feelings for him that I felt all those months ago but I could have cared less. I already had a good buzz on.

It had started to rain by the time we left "The Loop" and it was a full blown downpour by the time we got back to the hotel. Richie fumbled for the key which meant that we were completely soaked by the time we got into the room. My hair was wet all the way through, along with my dress which was now clinging to every curve of my body.

Richie did look kind of cute standing with his sandy colored hair soaked to his tanned skin. I don't know if it was the buzz I had from drinking or if I truly was seeing this guy differently. Either way, he looked pretty damn sexy.

It started to thunder and lightning, the rain pummeling the roof of the hotel. The winds were gusty and it almost felt as though our room was shaking. I love a good thunderstorm and this was an awesome one. I stared out the window watching the lightning flash across the sky.

I turned around just as another flash happened and saw Richie standing in the light of it, staring at me. His eyes were welling up with tears.

"I really am sorry that I hurt you. Really, I was such an asshole to do that to you. Please give me another chance," he pleaded, inching closer and closer to me. He placed his hands on my hips, jerking me back and forth a bit, "please, give me another chance! C'mon, do it, do it. Do it for me."

"Richie, I'm not angry anymore and I forgave you a long time ago but I don't know, I just don't know about this," and with that he kissed me long and hard and I fell for him all over again, and this time I fell right into the bed.

We made love for hours, coming up for air and a beer now and again.

I woke in Richie's arms in the morning, realizing that I had just given him what he wanted.

Me.

Chapter 21

John left for his appointments and, seeing that I had no agenda for the day other than to wait for his return, I finished my coffee and got back into bed, the bed that we had made love in only an hour or so ago. I turned on the news and slid down beneath the sheets. I rolled onto the pillow that John had rested his head on, his warmth, his smell still fresh on the sheets. I took a deep breath, slowly inhaling the scent of my lover. I closed my eyes and fell back into a light sleep, thinking about our night, our morning, our lovemaking. Just as I was about to drift into a deep sleep my cell phone rang, startling me out of the blissful state that I was sliding into. It rang a few times before I was awake enough to answer it. I reached for my phone and groggily answered. I was startled into a complete state of consciousness by the voice I heard as I said hello.

It was Richie.

"Good morning. It's almost ten o'clock and I'm guessing by how long it took you to answer the phone and by the tone of your voice that I woke you up. I've never known you to sleep past six. Guess Miami is making you lazy. Everything okay there?" he said with that condescending tone in his voice.

"Richie, oh, what time did you say it was?" I asked him in a sleepy tone of voice. If he only knew WHY I was so tired!

"I said it's ten o'clock! I'm guessing that you made it there in one piece. I don't remember getting the text you were supposed to send saying you got there ok but hey, you're on vacation, right?" he chided. I hated when he was like this but then again, he was like this a lot, a far cry from the husband that planted a kiss on my lips and hired a limo for me. I knew that time was short lived, it always was and truth be told, always will be.

"Sorry, the plane was fine. Looks like I've overcome my fear of flying because I absolutely loved it and would fly again in a heartbeat," I answered, knowing full well that I meant that I'd fly anywhere that John asked me to go. "How are the kids?"

"Kids are okay. Little guy missed you last night but he slept through the night. He's up and playing with his puzzles. The other two are off at school and I'm just wondering what to do first. The kids left a mess this morning," he said.

I could only imagine what the house looked like. On the rare occasion that I was sick and Richie was in charge, nothing got done. I had to get well quickly, if for no other reason than to put the house back together.

"Glad to see you like flying now. Sure opens up all sorts of possibilities for you, doesn't it? Is Colleen there yet?" he asked, his arrogance showing through and through.

Colleen, I thought, what? Oh, thank God I remembered the reason that I was in Miami in the first place.

"Oh, yeah, she got in before me but is out at her meeting right now. I'm going to rent a car and go sightseeing this afternoon. Listen, I want to hop in the shower and get moving. I'll call you later," I said.

"Sure, whatever you want. It's YOUR vacation. And hey, how did Colleen get to her meeting without a car?" he asked. Oh, shit, I hadn't thought of such details! Think fast, think fast, think REAL fast!

"There must have been a shuttle or something, I'm not sure. I was asleep when she left. Listen, I'll call you later, ok?" I said, hoping, no, PRAYING, that I sounded convincing.

"Okay, talk to you later," he said and we hung up the phone.

That was close, that was TOO close and I could feel my heart racing, then again, my heart had been racing from the moment that I saw John waiting for me at the top of the escalator last night.

I got up and out of bed and hopped into the shower. The hot water felt good against my skin and relaxed my muscles, the ones that were sore from my night of lovemaking with John. It was a good sore, though, and one I hadn't felt in what seemed like forever. I was sure that over the next few days I'd be quite used to moving in ways that I hadn't in years.

I washed my hair, shaved my legs and soaped up my body, the body that John had slid his soapy hands over last night. My mind drifted into thoughts of lying in the bathtub with him, his hands gently caressing my skin, slowly taking me to an excited and very happy state of mind.

My heart was missing him with an ache so deep that I could have cried, and my body, my soul, was yearning for his touch. How was I ever going to leave him in two days and go back home? I quickly put thoughts of what I'd have to deal with away and returned back to thinking of "now," of this time we have, just us.

There was no place in my mind now for Richie or the kids, so I directed my thoughts to that of only John and I, to fantasies of lovemaking and a life of he and I together. No spouses, no responsibilities.

A dream of mine? Yes, but one which I lived my life by day to day. A dream that saw me through my days at home, a dream that would help to pass the hours of the day until my lover came home to me for good.

After all, dreams can come true and a heart has a mind of its own.

I was missing John already and counting the hours until his return.

Richie and I began dating seriously after our trip to Atlantic City. He began to impress me more and more as time passed. He had his own business and always had a stack of cash in his pocket. We spent every weekend together, going to expensive restaurants, dancing at clubs until they closed and beaching it during the day.

Richie loved to surf and we'd spend all day at the surfing beach in Belmar. He'd surf and I'd lie on the beach, soaking up the sun and watching him. I was quite the dutiful girlfriend. Once in a while he'd coax me into going on the board with him but my fear of the water kept me from doing that very often. Surfing was his thing, lying on the beach watching him was mine.

In between tasty waves he'd come sit with me on my blanket, sliding his tan body next to mine. He'd reach his arm around my shoulder pulling me in close to kiss me, as though we were the only people on that beach, then he was back in the water.

Richie was a phenomenal lover. I'd let my wild imagination run free when I was with him, all to please HIM, which it did. I'd dress in sexy clothes which I kept at his house. I gave in to all his fantasies. Our sex life was a good one, though not the same as what John and I had in high school.

Yes, John and I were merely kids back then, and inexperienced as some would imagine, but with John it was different. It wasn't about fulfilling fantasies, it was about filling each other with love and with the essence of each other. We fit like a glove together.

Richie and I didn't fit like a glove, but it worked. We had a good sex life, though more filled with the physical aspect than the romantic. Still, that's how he wanted it. More physical, less emotional.

And I did just that.

All in all, our relationship was working and working well.

And through it all I found myself thinking less and less of John.

And more and more of Richie.

Chapter 22

I threw on a pair of jeans and a black Gap t-shirt, grabbed my pocketbook and headed for the hotel lobby where the rental car shuttle was waiting. I hopped on with another gentleman and struck up a casual conversation with him. It was just small talk to fill the ride to the rental car building which we were at within five minutes. We said goodbye, exchanging a quick "Enjoy your stay" and headed in our separate directions.

I approached the counter to find a woman in a blue uniform standing behind it. She was well groomed and looked to be about my mothers age. She looked up to me and flashed a smile, then said the standard line at all rental car counters, "Good morning, here to pick up or drop off?"

"I'm picking up," I said.

"Very well, then, what type of car are you looking to rent?" she asked, getting out all the necessary forms to be filled out.

"Something small," I answered, but then I stopped for a moment to think about it. Hmmm, should I or shouldn't I? What the hell, I thought, go for it.

"Do you have a convertible to rent?" I asked desperately hoping that she did.

"Actually you're in luck. I have a brand new Mustang convertible. How's that sound, honey?" she asked.

"Awesome, I've never driven one before. This is certainly a check off of my bucket list!" I answered excitedly. Look at that, me, ME, in a convertible. Who would have thought? Not Richie, I knew that for sure. He'd think I was silly and stupid, but I didn't care. This is what I wanted.

We proceeded to fill out the necessary papers and she picked up the phone and dialed someone to have them bring the car around for me. While we waited for the car she handed me a map of the city and explained the best way to drive a convertible.

"Put the top down and roll the windows up. It cuts down on the wind messing up your pretty hair," she joked.

"Okay, thanks. I'll keep that in mind," I chuckled with a smile. She pointed to the window and I turned to look. There was a brand new, bright red Mustang convertible parked out in front.

"You have fun now," she said as I left the building.

I walked out of the building directly to that beautiful, sexy little car that was mine for the next few days. The man who brought the car around showed me how to work the controls for the top, put it down for me and helped me into the driver's seat.

"You sure have a pretty day for a drive around Miami in this car, young lady. You have yourself a good time and welcome to Miami!" he said as I drove off.

And he was right, it "sure was a pretty day." It was blue skies and bright sunshine with just a hint of a warm breeze blowing. I could smell the salt air that was only minutes down the road.

Life was feeling wonderful today.

I got onto the highway and stepped on the gas, accelerating to a speed of 80 miles an hour, a speed I haven't driven at since having kids and driving a minivan.

"You know what?" I thought outloud, talking to myself, "To hell with keeping the windows up."

I wanted to FEEL this day so I rolled them all down and let the Miami wind take hold of my hair, blowing it in all different directions. I felt free sailing down the highway, the sun beaming down on me, the wind dancing through my hair. It was a sense of freedom that I can't ever remember having felt. Maybe I never did.

And this was exactly what I needed.

I turned on the radio and fiddled with the buttons to find a classic rock station.

As luck would have it, I found one that was playing one of my favorite Fleetwood Mac songs...

> "Something in you brought out something in me
> That I've never been since."

It's the song that had just the perfect lyrics that described my life with John since rekindling our love affair.

I drove around for hours, free as a bird. I parked down by the beach, grabbed an iced coffee and took in the sights and sounds. I inhaled the scent of the salt air and closed my eyes to listen to the sounds of the waves crashing on the beach.

It was beautiful here. I was relaxed and felt at peace.

I didn't have anything to eat, not knowing what plans John had for dinner. I sat there in my convertible for an hour listening to the radio and drinking my iced coffee. This was definitely turning out to be a great day for me, right from my morning "wake up" call with John to the freedom of being alone and driving this sexy car under a gorgeous sky.

Right now I feel a million miles from home...

And from the life that was waiting for me there.

It was almost our one year anniversary and Richie had been acting strangely all week. He'd call me but wouldn't say much. I was beginning to wonder what was going on, just like I had over a year ago. Was this going to be another "I don't love you anymore, I love someone else moment?" I was getting myself ready to hear that since it seemed to be a pattern with him.

I was so stressed by Friday over his behavior that I left work early with a terrible migraine. I went straight home and into bed, knowing that Richie always came for dinner on Friday nights.

My phone rang about six o'clock, waking me up from my "nap" which lasted far longer than I had planned.

"Hey, let's go to the surfing beach," he said, still with that strange tone in his voice.

"I'm really not feeling too good. Bad headache and you actually just woke me up. And I don't feel like watching you surf today. Another time," I said, but he cut me off immediately in mid sentence.

"No, we HAVE to go. You'll be fine once you get out into the salt air. Get dressed and I'll be there in a half hour," he said, quite forcefully.

"Richie, I really don't want to. I don't feel that good," I said adamantly.

"You'll want to go, I just know it. See you soon," he said and with that he hung up the phone. Great, just great. My head hurts, my hair is flat from sleeping on it and my mouth tastes like I've been out drinking all night, but no, Richie speaks and I jump. What else is new?

I got out of bed and threw on my jeans and a hoodie sweatshirt. The nights were getting cooler this time of year, especially at the beach.

"Dammit," I thought to myself, "this is the last thing I feel like doing."

I brushed my teeth and tried to fix my hair. I checked my makeup in the mirror and it looked like someone had smeared it with a dishrag. Honestly, the things I do for him! I wiped a bit of my makeup off and tried to reapply what I could. I will say, it looked better.

I went downstairs to find a little bit of coffee left. It must have been sitting there since the afternoon because it tasted terrible but I needed a jolt of caffeine so I suffered through it.

I sat down on the couch, my hand holding my right temple which was throbbing mildly now. I closed my eyes and tried to think the pain away.

The next thing I knew Richie was walking through the front door. He looked pretty nice tonight. Jeans, surfer shirt and his Van sneakers.

"Let's go," he said anxiously and when I didn't get up off the couch as quickly as he had wanted me to he said, "NOW! C'mon!"

"Geez, take it down a notch. I'm coming, I'm coming," I said, starting to feel annoyed.

He hurried me out the door and into his car. He had disco music playing which I loved and he hated. What's going on? My head hurt and I just wanted to get on with whatever the hell was going on.

We drove straight down to the surfing beach. He hopped out of the car and took a blanket out from the backseat.

"C'mon, let's walk down on the beach," he said excitedly. I got out, grabbed his hand and let him lead me down to the beach. He put the blanket down and we sat together, holding hands.

We sat there in silence for what seemed like forever but was probably just about 10 minutes. No words. No conversation. Nothing.

"C'mon, Richie," I thought to myself, "what the hell is going on?"

Suddenly he grabbed my hands and looked into my eyes.

"I love you and want to spend the rest of my life with you. Will you marry me?" and with that he pulled out an engagement ring. I was stunned to say the least because Richie never believed in marriage. He swore he'd never do it and here he was, on the surfing beach, asking me to marry him. Words escaped me.

"Well?" he asked. He was beginning to look nervous, as if I'd say no, but I didn't. I gave him a big YES and threw my arms around him. I started to cry and said, "Yes!" over and over to him as if to make sure he heard me or understood what I was saying.

I was so happy and was beginning to realize that this is a dream that I'd had since I was a little girl, to grow up, get married and have children. My God, I thought, I'M GETTING MARRIED!

We kissed and hugged for a while before we decided to leave and make our rounds of telling my family. My parents were first on the list.

We walked hand in hand off of the beach, got back into the car and headed to my house. My life was about to change and I was about to commit myself to Richie until death due us part.

I was certain now that I'd live happily ever after.

But I was wondering why at the exact moment I said yes to Richie, John came to mind.

Chapter 23

It was getting late in the afternoon so I decided to head back to the hotel. I was certain that I would need some big time freshening up before John got back home.

And I was right because when I got back to the room and looked in the mirror my hair looked as though it had been in a hurricane that I barely survived! I guess riding around in Miami with the top down was similar to driving around in a hurricane, at least where your hair is concerned.

I brushed it all back into place, quite pleased with the fact that I didn't have to rewash it and blow dry it all over again. My makeup survived the windy drive fairly well with only a minor touch up needed. It was nearly four o'clock and I knew that John would be back soon so I took inventory of the clothes I had brought and opted for a tight, white tank top. It wasn't too sheer, but tight enough that John would definitely be able to see and feel my excitement through it.

I walked down the hall to grab a couple of sodas and some ice and headed back to the room to give a quick call home to Richie.

I grabbed my cell and hit his number. He answered by the fourth ring.

"How's it going?" I asked when he answered.

"And a hello to you, too! Everything's fine here. How's Miami?" he asked.

"It's great. I rented a Mustang convertible. Cool, huh?" I said excitedly.

"That's such a trashy car. Why'd you do that?" he asked arrogantly.

I was glad that the asshole in him reared its ugly head every so often. It enabled me to be an adultress much more easily than if it didn't.

"It is not," I said angrily, but just as I said that I heard the key in the door and John was walking through. I motioned to him to stay quiet and mouthed to him that it was Richie on the phone. He stayed quiet as he sat down on the bed next to me.

I continued a tense conversation with Richie about the kids with John sitting right next to me. He was chatting endlessly about nothing in particular, which is typical, when John looked at me with a very devilish look in his eye. He took his fingertip and started rubbing it across my nipples. They started to get hard with excitement and were very pronounced through my white shirt. My mind was becoming dizzy as I tried to concentrate on the conversation with Richie on the phone. John lifted my shirt up and began sucking on my nipples, sending me into a delirious state of mind.

"Are you listening to me?" an annoyed Richie said.

Am I listening? No, I am not. I am feeling as though I want to jump the man that's arousing me and make love to him here and now.

"Yeah, but let me go. I'm hungry and Colleen will be here soon so that we can grab dinner," I said.

And by God, was I hungry, just not for food.

"Good bye then," Richie said and hung up abruptly. I could have cared less how he felt about now. I knew how I was feeling, which was excited and horny beyond belief.

"You feeling good, babe?" John asked in between little licks of my now hard nipples.

"You are so bad! I'll show you just how good I feel," I said as I lifted off my shirt and pressed his body down onto the bed. I unbuttoned his shirt, then his pants. I slid my hand down into his pants and grabbed onto him, tight.

"How's THAT feel?" I asked, knowing full well by the size of him just how he felt. He started to shift on the bed, his pants constricting the enormity of his erection. I slid his pants down around his ankles, grabbing his shoes off then taking his pants off completely.

I slid my pants off and straddled him while he lay on the bed.

"What's your pleasure, sir?" I asked, sounding like an airline attendant.

"Oh, baby, you know what my pleasure is!" and with that I smiled and as John would say, "I headed south!" I pleasured him with my mouth, the sounds of his excitement bringing me to a place of excitement all of my own. He exploded in my mouth and I savored all the love he had to offer me. I moved back up to him and kissed him over and over.

"I love you so much. Don't you ever leave me!" he said and I think he surprised even himself by what he had just professed out loud.

He knew that I'd never leave him. He had to know that by now.

I let him rest for a few minutes and I got dressed, yet again.

"So, what's the dinner plans?" I asked while putting on my shoes.

"Oh, yeah, dinner," he answered, his mind slowly drifting back into reality.

"Dinner, right, we're eating out. Outside that is. We'll take my car."

"Ok. Wait, I forgot to tell you that I rented a convertible. Let's take MY car!" I wondered if he thought that this was a trashy car like Richie did.

"Are you kidding me, babe? That's fucking cool! I love convertibles even though I've never owned one. In fact, that gives me a great idea! Let me change and we'll head out!" he said.

Unlike Richie, he thought this was cool.

John was dressed in a few minutes and we headed out the door and into the Mustang. I handed him the keys and off we drove, the top down and the music blaring. We decided to head to the beach and grab some takeout to eat in the car by the water.

We parked and realized that the world was our oyster when it came to choices of takeout food!

We hopped out of the car and started strolling along the water, looking to see if one particular restaurant jumped out at us.

"PIZZA!" John yelled. He loved pizza although I was a bit less excited than him about it. My love for pizza was not as strong as his, let's just say, but my love for him was stronger and I could certainly muster up the excitement for pizza if that's what he wanted.

John ordered a pizza with everything on it. While we were waiting for it to be done we found a liquor store nearby and stopped and picked up two bottles of wine, along with a corkscrew.

We grabbed the pizza along with two empty cups and headed back to the car. We jumped into the back seat and John opened the first bottle of wine, pouring it into the empty cups that we got from the pizza place. Such romance!

Our "dinner out" has begun, and even though it's not what I had imagined, it was the perfect night. Any night, anywhere, with John was perfect.

John wolfed down half the pizza, washing it down with a glass of wine.

I, on the other hand, ate like a teenage girl on her first date: one slice of pizza, wiping my mouth off after every bite, and small sips of wine.

"Babe, we have two bottles of wine that I intend on killing before we go home. Drink up, love!" he said and with that, I filled the cup with wine and began to drink it down.

I thought that John would never get done eating, but he finally did after savoring every single bite. He cleaned up the car and we sat back with our wine to do some "people watching" and to stare up at the stars. And what could make this night even more romantic? A full moon.

And we watched it rise above the water.

It was a bright, orange ball that showed itself on the horizon and we watched as it climbed higher and higher, its orange color reflecting on the water. It was absolutely stunning.

We were talking about ourselves and our kids. It's as though Richie and his wife, Tess, were the two topics that we never discussed and I was glad for that. The stars were out in full force, something that I'm sure John must have arranged just for me.

John put his arm around me and I snuggled deep into his shoulder, savoring every moment like this that I had with him. I fit perfectly on his chest. It's as if our bodies were made to be a perfect match for one another. We certainly did fit each other like a glove.

I knew our time together was halfway over and I wanted my heart to capture every single moment.

And it did.

My heart took picture after picture.

It was nearing ten o'clock when we decided to head back to the hotel. We climbed back into the front seat and drove off, holding hands throughout the drive back. John parked the car and we walked back into the hotel, arm in arm.

We were home.

I grabbed two glasses of wine at the lobby bar and took them up to the room with us. We hadn't finished all of the wine we had bought so we decided to finish it up in our room after these two glasses.

We each sat down in a chair by the window, feet up on the ottoman. John and I began to drink the glasses of wine I had brought up from downstairs. At least we had glasses to drink our 2nd bottle of wine out of instead of paper cups from a pizza joint!

"I have to call home, babe. I'll be back in a little while," he said as he walked out the door. I hated that, hated that he wouldn't call home with me in the room. I did it, why couldn't he? He was all over my body when I was on the phone with Richie, what's the deal with Tess? What was he saying to her that I couldn't hear? I love you?

Once again, John get's what John wants.

And I give it to him every time.

I gulped down the first glass of wine and poured the second. Fifteen minutes had passed by, now it was twenty. I was getting angrier by the minute. I finished my second glass and decided to go down to the lobby bar and get another one.

Except this time I drank it at the bar.

Alone.

I was halfway through my third glass when I saw John walking through the lobby looking for me. I felt a little drunk and very put off. He found me at the bar and took me by the arm back to the elevator.

We got back to MY room, no words spoken between us the entire elevator ride. I was upset and I'm certain that he knew it.

And if he didn't he was a fool.

Our wedding day was here and I woke up with stars in my eyes. Finally, I would be married. Richie's friends were doubtful that he would actually go through with it. They kept telling me that, yes, while it was a fact that we were engaged, that indeed Richie was a confirmed bachelor. In his group of friends he was the one they would have put money on that would never get married, and they were still holding to that fact.

Yet here we were, Richie clad in a handsome, black tux, standing with Ted, his best man, in the church office. I was in the sanctuary foyer, clad in the wedding gown of my dreams, puffy white sleeves with lots of lace and pearls, a sweet little white hat with a beautiful shoulder length veil.

Colleen and my sister were at my side dressed in tea length teal bridesmaids gowns, matching hats and veils adorning their perfectly coiffed heads. Everything was in place and the music was starting. Colleen peaked into the church.

"Richie and Ted are up front! It's time!" she said excitedly. I felt my palms starting to sweat and I was starting to get nervous, not at the thought of marriage but at the thought of two hundred people staring at me as my Dad walked me down the aisle.

What if I fainted or tripped?

Too late now, besides that, marriage and the man I loved were waiting at the front of the church for me and I have waited all my life for this. I figured that if I actually did faint or trip they could just drag me up the aisle to Richie.

The bridesmaids started up the aisle, one by one, until I heard "The Wedding March" begin to play.

It was time.

"Ready?" my Dad asked nervously. I think he was just as afraid to trip as I was.

"I've been ready all my life, Pop," I said and with that I took his arm and my father walked me down the aisle to Richie, the man who was about to take his daughter away from him.

My father practically ran me down the aisle but thankfully neither of us tripped or fainted. He kissed me on the cheek.

And then he gave me away to Richie.

It was a short, traditional ceremony and within fifteen minutes I went from being a single girl to a married woman. The organ started playing music and my "husband" took my arm for the first time as his wife and led me down the aisle to the back of the church where we formed our reception line.

The bridal party followed, showering us with hugs and kisses. The guys were giving Richie pats on the back followed with "Wait 'til tonight, buddy! That's where the fun begins!"

Men. Their minds can never get out of that gutter.

I didn't care, though.

I was deliriously happy right now and as far as I was concerned, Richie was all mine.

He was my husband.

"My husband!"

Those were the words that I had dreamed of hearing since I was a little girl.

This was our wedding day, my wedding day, it was my dream of a life of happiness and love which, in time, would turn out to be just that, "a dream."

Because deep inside of me I realized that in my mind it was John that I had just married.

Chapter 24

"What the hell is the matter with you? Are you drunk?" John asked, sounding extremely annoyed.

"Do you love me?" I asked him. "Are you IN love with me?" I asked, sounding just as annoyed as he did.

"What the hell is that supposed to mean? Why would you even ask that? Of course I love you. Why do you think I'm here with YOU?" he said angrily. And he definitely was angry. In fact, I had never heard him angry before and I was starting to feel nervous, but I was too far into this to back down now. I was hoping that I hadn't ruined anything or worse, ruined "us."

"I know that you love me but are you IN love with me?" I shot back. Now I was feeling less annoyed and more angry.

"Don't be ridiculous, there's no difference. Love is love," he said back to me with more annoyance in his voice than I was comfortable with.

"Why don't you ever call Tess with me in the room? You've been with me when I've talked with Richie, hell, you've even messed around with me while I'm on the phone with him. Or did you forget that? What's all the secrecy about? Are you telling her that you love her or something? Do you miss her? Are you sleeping with her while you're sleeping with me? Answer me, dammit. Say something," I yelled at him. The wine had definitely caused me to lose sense of how loud my voice was.

John just sat there. I wasn't sure if he was thinking of what to say or if he was so mad at me that he couldn't answer. Either way I was beginning to think that I may have gone too far.

Or not far enough.

I always give John what he wants when he wants it. Now it's my turn. I want answers. I want to know if it's me or her.

And I want to know if he's going to break my heart.

The sound of silence in our room, or by now I was feeling as though it was just MY room, was deafening, and now I was scared. I used my voice to tell him how I was feeling and asked him questions that I needed answered.

But I guess in an affair you don't have those rights. You aren't allowed to become a burden. You aren't allowed to use your voice. You aren't allowed to feel any emotion other than the ones that they want you to feel.

And that's not fair.

I left my husband and kids to be with him. I lied through my teeth. I'm being everything that John wants, giving him everything that he wants, so don't I have any rights in this relationship?

Or is it truly just a torrid affair?

Is it that he's never planned on leaving his wife?

Is this just a fun thing for him or is it real?

My head was swimming with one thought after another and I was also starting to feel sick. Maybe it was too much wine, too much pizza, or too much John.

I was about to find out, that I knew with certainty.

"I think I should sleep in my room tonight," he said. Oh, God, now I did it. I broke the rules that I didn't even know were in place. I could feel myself starting to back down and I was scared to death.

"John, please, I just needed to ask you these things. These aren't things to be asked over the phone or in texts or emails. I'm sorry that I upset you. It's the wine, really, babe, it's the wine. I'm sorry. I just get scared sometimes. I just don't know why you won't call her with me around. Please, I'm begging you, please don't be mad at me," I said, pleading for my life, or my heart at least. I didn't want to lose him and was afraid that I went too far, even though it was the truth of how I felt and what I needed to say, what I needed to ask.

"I don't know what to say. I'm here, with you, and you know that I love you. I don't know why I call her away from you. I just thought it would be uncomfortable for you to hear me on the phone with her. And no, I'm not sleeping with her. I've told you that before," he said angrily.

"Where the hell did all of this come from? We've been having a great time together and you seem to be hell bent on ruining it. If you don't trust me then we don't have much going for us," John said in a tone that was completely foreign to me. He had never spoken to me in this tone before and I was sure that I had ruined what we had.

"I'm sorry, I'm sorry," I said through tears that were now flowing down my face. I tried to hug him but he pulled away from me. His body was stiff and he just sat there angry and looking at me as though I'd just broken his heart.

"John, please, please understand. It's the wine talking, really. I don't usually drink that much. Don't be this way towards me. I love you and I'm sorry. Please, can't we just forget it, babe?" I asked, trying my hardest to change his mind and his mood. I was beginning to sound desperate and I didn't like it.

"I can't forget this one. And screw your fucking wine excuse, this is YOU talking, or should I say bitching! You said how you felt and now I'm trying to deal with it and with you. Just leave it be. I need to think things through," he said as he lit a cigarette and moved to the chair across the room from me.

I was feeling angry at myself for having drank so much wine. Yes, it was true, I was angry and needed to tell him how I felt. After all, he left me sitting alone in our room for almost a half hour after such a beautiful night out.

I'm sure that the wine added extra anger and emotion to the whole situation but the truth is, HE caused the situation by leaving me alone. His wife will have him soon enough all to herself. Why can't she just leave him alone while he's with me?

We only have tonight and tomorrow night left together and I just single handedly screwed it all up. What the hell was I thinking?

Actually, I was thinking of ME and that is something I'm not used to doing. After years of marriage to Richie I learned never to voice an opinion or upset the apple cart.

Yet didn't I count? Didn't my opinion matter? Weren't my feelings valid?

I threw "me" out the window and walked towards John.

"Please, babe, please stay with me tonight. Please don't leave. We don't have much time left together before we go home. I'm sorry. I'm so sorry. It's all my fault," I said, sobering up pretty damn quick.

And that is the girl that I was used to being. The girl who felt as though everything was her fault and that she didn't matter. The girl who took the abuse and apologized for the abuser.

But John mattered more to me than my own life.

"I don't know. I'm not feeling in the mood at the moment," he said. "I'm going to my room to think about it. If I don't show up within the hour, that means I'm not coming back." My heart broke.

"Please…" I begged.

"Stop. You're embarrassing yourself. I'm going to my room to think about whether or not I want to come back and if I do, this conversation of crazy questions ends here, okay?" he said, still sounding annoyed and like a man taking control of the situation and of me.

"Okay," I said, completely defeated.

He left me alone in my room for the second time tonight. I wasn't sure if he would come back. Was he playing with my heart? Was he screwing with my mind?

I laid down on the bed and cried. I ruined everything.

It was getting late and I was tired and starting to feel the after effects of the wine. My head was starting to hurt and my heart felt as though it were breaking. I went into the bathroom, took two of my headache pills and put on my pajamas. I washed my face, brushed my teeth and slid into bed…alone.

It had been almost an hour since John walked out and I figured that this was going to be my punishment. He was going to leave me alone for the night.

Just as I was leaning over to turn off the light the door opened and John walked in.

"You're wearing pajamas tonight? That's just great," he said with an annoyed sarcasm in his voice.

"I'm staying. Seriously, you didn't think I'd come back? You need to have a little more faith in me and trust, if that's an option," he said as he began to undress, get naked and slide into bed next to me.

"Let's watch a movie, babe, it's been a long day," he said. I took my pajamas off, threw them to the floor and laid my head on his chest. He didn't offer me his arm as he usually does but he didn't push me away either. I guess that was a good sign. It was something.

He found a movie and purchased it. He sat up in bed which forced me to move over. He lit another cigarette and I had one with him but there was no conversation between us.

I started to watch the movie with him but soon fell asleep, partially from the fight, partially from the wine, and partially from my headache pills.

John and I didn't make love that night.

We didn't do anything that night.

Our first few months of marital bliss was cut short by the death of Richie's mother, followed shortly afterwards by the death of my grandmother. It was a terribly sad time for both of us.

Richie started to keep to himself a bit more, surfing weekends without me, staying up hours after I went to bed and having no conversation at all with me. We were both working full time yet while I spent my weekends cleaning the house, food shopping and doing laundry, he was busy having a good time without me.

He began going out on weekend nights until well after the bars closed. I could feel a change in our relationship, as if a dark cloud had taken residence over our lives. He dismissed each and every conversation I tried to engage in with him to explain how I was feeling. I wanted to tell him that we were still newlyweds and I felt as though he wasn't even in a relationship with me anymore, let alone a marriage. He shut me down every single time. I felt helpless.

And terrified.

Our sex life certainly wasn't the same as it was before we were married, occurring less and less frequently. It was as if all the romance and excitement died on our wedding day.

Had marriage changed him?

I was beginning to think that now was a good time to talk about starting a family. Surely, I thought, this would bring us closer and make the marriage better. I approached the subject with Richie one Friday night after dinner.

"We haven't even been married a year now and you want a baby? It's too soon," he said as if that would end the conversation.

"I think it'd be good for us, Richie. Just think, a child, our child, a little piece of you and a little piece of me. Can't you imagine how great that would be?" I asked, trying desperately to say the right things to persuade him into agreeing with me.

"You're romanticizing the whole damn thing. Think of the work, not to mention what it means for us. Why can't things ever be enough for you? You always want more. You always NEED more!" he said with anger in his voice.

All I could think of at that moment was "How much further apart could we be from each other? I thought a baby would bring us closer."

"Please, Richie. I think it would be good for us. You'll see. It'll be great!" I said, smiling ear to ear, as if he would catch a piece of it.

"Fine, I might as well say yes now otherwise you'll just mope around until you get your way," he said annoyed. I didn't appreciate that he "gave in" to me, but at this point it was something and I would take whatever I could get from him.

"Thanks, honey, want to start trying now?" I said with all the charm of a woman who wanted to make love.

"No," he said matter of factly and went to bed.

I fell asleep on the couch with tears streaming down my face.

This wasn't the way I wanted things to be.

Where had my husband gone and would he ever come back to me?

As I fell into a deep sleep my dreams weren't of a baby with my husband, it was a dream of a baby with John.

Chapter 25

Morning came much too quickly and just as I had suspected, I had a hangover. My head felt as though it would explode. I turned to snuggle into John but he wasn't next to me. There was no aroma of fresh brewed coffee, no scent of his cologne, no cloud of smoke from his morning cigarette.

There was no sign of John.

I rolled back into my pillow and began to cry. He left me, I thought, he left me. And it was all my fault. Why was I so stupid last night? Why did I have to push him too far? Why? Why? Why?

Why was I "me?"

All of my life I had been told that it was "me," that everything was "my" fault.

At that moment I heard the key in the door and it opened. I rolled over, bleary eyed, and saw him standing there, laptop case in hand, dressed in a suit and tie, ready for his appointments.

"I thought you might need your sleep this morning so I showered in my room. I have to get going. I'll see you later today," he said coldly.

"John, I'm begging you, please don't stay mad at me. How many more times can I apologize to you? I really am sorry!" I said as I rose from the bed. I put my bathrobe on this time, certain that he wasn't in the mood for my naked body to be pressed up against his.

"I need to get to work. Just leave it all be for now. My mood will pass, just give it some time," he said.

But we don't have time, I thought to myself, tonight is our last night together. Time is one precious commodity that we don't have the luxury to have.

No affair does.

He walked over to me and kissed me goodbye. I pulled him back and wrapped my arms around him. He put just one of his arms back around me, still holding his computer with the other.

It was the coldest embrace that I ever felt.

"John…" my voice trailed off.

"I love you, but you need to let it go today, okay? Can you do that please?" he said as he pulled away from me.

"I'll see you later. I should be done pretty early today, probably around two or so. I'll see you then," he said and with that he walked through the door and left.

I stood there and watched him leave.

It wasn't just my room that he was walking out of, I felt that he was walking out of my life, as well.

Our son, Billy, was born about a year after Richie and I had started trying to get pregnant. Just as I had suspected, the pregnancy brought us closer together. He was wonderful during my pregnancy, waiting on me hand and foot, taking pictures of my monthly "belly growth." He was by my side the minute my water broke and stayed there until our sweet son burst into the world.

Richie was pleased as could be at having a son. He changed his first diaper in the hospital and brought him to me to nurse when he was hungry.

He decorated our home all in blue for the day we came home from the hospital. It looked so beautiful as I walked through our front door with our brand new baby boy and it warmed my heart to see the lengths that he had gone to for me to make me happy.

And I was happier than I had been in my whole life.

Life seemed to be back to the way it was when we were first married. We had found each other again and now had a precious son between us to share.

We took Billy everywhere with us, road trips, the beach, the mall. Wherever we went, Billy was with us. We were a threesome now, a real family and I was happy.

Billy filled the hole in my heart that I felt when Richie drifted away from me and now he had come back to me.

Our second child, Katie, was born four years later and once again, Richie was thrilled. She was definitely "Daddy's girl" for sure and he loved that. We had such a sweet little family growing amongst us that I thought that life just couldn't get any better, or any worse.

Our third child, Jonah, was born two years later and once again, he felt like the superior male having two sons!

Richie and I were doing okay but things were beginning to change. We had moved into our new home right after Katie was born. It was a small Cape Cod, so when Jonah arrived we were living in tight quarters. Richie began sleeping on the couch every night, leaving me alone upstairs with two toddlers and an infant. He told me that it was because the baby's crying kept him up all night and that someone had to go to work in the morning to pay for his family, and reminded me that that someone was "him."

"I know that, honey. It's a lot of work taking care of three kids and I'm grateful that I'm home with them. I really am and I'm grateful that you are the one going to work everyday so that we can have this life together," I said, sounding like a woman who was simply desperate to have her husband back again.

"Then you shouldn't be upset or surprised that I need my sleep and can't get it with the baby crying all through the night. Stop being so selfish. Do you want me to quit my job and stay home with the kids and you can go to work?" he said sarcastically.

"No, that's not what I'm saying. Do what you have to do. I don't want to fight. Sleep on the couch if you need to. I understand," I said in defeat. I was not going to make him understand. I learned throughout our years of marriage so far that it was easier to give in to him and back down.

It's a cycle that I was a pro at.

"Good. Glad you get it. It only took an hour to get you to understand that it's you with the problem, not me," he said arrogantly.

And with that he laid back on the coach and I went back upstairs to bed.

Deep down inside I knew that there was more going on. It wasn't just the baby crying, especially since he didn't cry all night. No, there was something more going on in Richie's life, a life that he was living without me and the kids.

He ended up coming home late from work every night and began going out on Friday and Saturday nights.

"What, I can't go out with friends?" he asked with a snappy tone in his voice.

"I didn't say that, but you're married and we have kids here. I'd like to see you more, spend time with you," I said, as if pleading my case.

"So I work over 40 hours a week, not getting home until late at night and I don't deserve some time out? Some fun?" he said knowing that once again I'd soon give in and he'd get his way.

"That's not what I meant and yes, you deserve some time. Don't I deserve some time, too? At least a night out with my husband?" I asked boldly.

"What do you want from me? I pay for everything, I don't ask you for anything. You wanted these kids, now you want more?" he yelled.

"No, I don't want MORE. I just want you. More YOU!" I answered matter of factly.

"Well, be happy with the kids because right now I'm stretched so far with work that I need my own time alone with my friends, not trapped in a small house bursting at the seams with kids…and you," he said.

"Honey, I'm sorry. I just miss you but I understand you need space from all of us," I conceded.

"Good," he answered with a tone in his voice that signaled the end of this discussion.

Time marched on and Richie ended up becoming even more distant from me and the kids. I was coming to terms with my "absentee husband" and began to care less and less about what he did. He continued with his new lifestyle, forging ahead with new interests and new friends. Our marriage and children had taken a back seat to his "freedom."

I missed him and tried every so often to fix things between us, but you can't fix a marriage alone. It took the two of us to break it and would need the two of us to fix it.

And right now, there seemed to be only one of us left.

I stopped caring about a marriage that was already over and threw all my energy into the kids. Motherhood was all that I was interested in right now.

I just never thought that my marriage would suffer from it.

Chapter 26

I felt so lost after John left, uncertain of what the outcome of this "disagreement" would be. My head still hurt but my heart felt worse. I ordered up some coffee and a bagel from room service and ate alone, something that I didn't relish on this trip.

I missed seeing his face across the table as we talked over breakfast together, laughing and giggling as if this were a normal, everyday routine for us. I missed sending him off with a big kiss and a pat on his cute little bottom, wishing him with all sincerity to have a great day. I missed the twinkle in his eye when he said "see 'ya later, babe."

Now I wasn't sure where I stood with him and I certainly didn't like where I was standing at this moment.

I decided to take a quick drive around town, hoping that some fresh, salty sea air would help to alleviate my migraine. The day was warm, but not as sunny as it had been. I believe it was a prelude to the rainy day that was predicted for tomorrow, our last day together.

I turned on the radio and caught wind of a James Taylor song. The lyrics resonated through my mind as he sang "shower the people you love with love, show them the way that you feel."

And that's exactly what I wanted to do to John as I listened to that song.

I wanted nothing more than to shower John with all the love that I had in my heart for him.

The winds were beginning to pick up so I decided to head back to the hotel and grab a salad there to eat in my room. My mind was wondering if it was MY room or OUR room, just as it was on that first night.

It was about one o'clock so I decided to close the curtains and watch a bit of television. The skies were turning darker and it was beginning to look as though the rain predicted for tomorrow was going to show itself today.

I scrolled through the channels and found nothing of interest so I decided to turn it off and take a nap. I needed to do something to shut off the thoughts racing through my mind.

I don't know how long I was asleep begore I was woken up by a pair of lips kissing behind my ear. I smiled. It was John and I was hoping that this kiss meant that everything was alright. That WE were alright.

I started to sit up when he said, "Shhh, don't get up. I'm tired too, babe, so let's just take a nap together. I think we could both use it, don't you?" he asked.

And with that my sweet boy curled up into my back, our favorite "spooning" position and wrapped his arms around me. We fell into a deep, blissful sleep together.

An hour or so passed when my eyes started to open. It was dark in the room, a darkness caused by more than the closed curtains. I could hear the rolls of thunder and see the brief flashes of lightning through the crack in the center of the curtain where it wasn't closed all the way.

John was in a deep sleep, snoring as usual. I slid carefully out of his arms trying not to wake him. I got up and ordered a pot of coffee from room service, noting that it was almost six o'clock. We definitely slept with the angels for the last several hours.

The coffee was at the door within ten minutes and I'm sure it was the knock on the door from room service that woke John up. He rolled onto his back and yawned, his arms outstretched above his head.

"Hey, babe," he said sleepily as he slid up into a sitting position, adjusting the pillows behind him.

I made each of us a cup of coffee and sat down on the edge of the bed. I started to hand John his cup but he took both his and my cup and set them down on the nightstand. He grabbed my hand and pulled me down onto the bed with him, sitting me down onto his lap. He cupped my face in his hands and kissed me softly on the lips.

"How could you ever doubt me, babe? I love you so much and would never leave you, ever," he said convincingly. He looked into my eyes and once again my heart melted. I began to cry. Soft tears rolled down my cheeks.

"I know you love me, but you left me once before. It scares the hell out of me to think that that could happen again. You need to understand that it's almost unreal to me to believe that anyone could love me the way that you do. It's not that I doubt you, it's more that I doubt that anyone could ever love me like this," I said, nuzzling the side of his neck, a dangerous erotic zone of John's, one that I was well acquainted with. One that I knew as to where it would lead.

He took me by the shoulders and pulled me back to stare directly into my face.

"I will NEVER leave you again. I've sorted everything out in my mind and I know that what we have is real and right. Trust me and don't ever think that someone couldn't love you in the way that you want or deserve. I love you more than anyone. I always have and always will," he said with a softness in his tone that I was grateful to hear.

"Sure, babe, I love Tess just as you love Richie, but we'll never love either of them the way that we love each other. You have to believe that. You just have to. And you can't ever doubt me. It makes me feel bad about myself to think that you could. This is the real thing, we just happen to have other commitments at the moment, that's all," he said trying to convince me and himself, I'm sure.

"This, what we have right here, right now, is the real thing. You and me and together we can do anything. We'll make this work for as long as we need to. Trust me. Please, trust me," John said taking me back into his arms

"I do trust you, John, and I promise that I'll never doubt you again. I mean that, love," I said, kissing the shoulder that my head was now buried onto.

"Everything is fine between us. In fact, it's more than fine, it's great. Now, let's put last night in the past and savor our last night together. I want to love you with all that I am tonight. I want you to know tonight, more than any other night, just how much you mean to me and just how incredibly much I love you," he said with all the passion that a man who was deeply in love with a woman could say.

I believed him and promised myself that I would never, ever again doubt the man who I'd change my whole life for.

That is, if he asked.

We drank our coffee, all snuggled up into bed and decided to have dinner in OUR room for the last night together. It took almost an hour for two steaks, two baked potatoes and two salads to arrive, but we didn't seem to notice, or for that matter, even seem to care. We were happy to be sitting together in each other's arms until it arrived.

I ran into the bathroom to freshen up and while I was doing that John must have placed another call to room service because when our dinner did arrive it came with candles, fresh flowers and two bottles of my favorite wine.

Wow, I stood there in disbelief that someone could do something so romantic and sweet for me. No one ever had before.

"Nice touch, babe," I said to him with a smile. God, he was good. He was REAL good. We dined by candlelight and listened to soft music while we ate and drank. It was the most beautiful meal for our last night together. I could only imagine how he could top this.

And top it he did.

We finished dinner and had a cigarette on the balcony, watching the remnants of the Florida storm that had blown by. John brought a bottle of wine outside with us and we sat there together, smoking and enjoying the wine.

"I'm going to take a shower," I said to John.

"You're taking a shower NOW?" he asked, looking puzzled.

I looked directly into his eyes and said, "No, WE'RE taking a shower. Be a good boy and help me undress," I said, knowing that I had plans of my own.

And he was a good boy because he jumped up from the chair and followed me into the bathroom. I could hear the music playing and started swaying back and forth, dancing for him as he took each piece of clothing off of my body.

I grabbed his hips and started moving back and forth. I slipped his shirt off first, then unzipped his pants, sliding them and his boxers down to his ankles all at once. We were two naked bodies moving in rhythm against one another to the music in a bathroom filled with steam from the hot shower.

At least I thought it was from the shower.

We danced together naked, our bodies entwined, hands grabbing onto each other's bottoms. I grabbed John's hand and led him into the shower.

I got wet first, the water running over me, soaking my hair. His fingers ran through the wet strands, pulling it back from my face. I pulled him close towards me so that the steady stream of hot water was pouring over both of our bodies.

I turned him around and soaped up his back, massaging his shoulders and arms, running my hands all over the back of him, straight down to his bottom. My hands reached around to the front of him, rubbing his belly, then his hips, the tops of his thighs, then gently, ever so gently, I soaped up the erection that my strokes had evoked in him. His head slid back and onto my shoulder and I kissed his neck.

He turned slowly, soaping his hands into a lather. As he looked into my eyes he massaged my shoulders, then my arms, then my breasts. His hands moved down slowly towards my hips then around me to my bottom. He stopped for only a moment to lather his hands up again, then continued his task of massaging me. He turned my body around and massaged my back, sliding his hands around to my front, caressing my breasts again, this time pulling at my nipples until they stood erect. His hands slid down to my belly, then a bit lower to the spot which was about to lose all control from his touch.

We continued this "dance" in the shower until John said, "I want to make love to you right in this shower."

Within seconds he was entering me from behind, the water gently beating down on us as we began a rhythmic dance together. John was kissing my shoulder as he thrust deeper and deeper into me, harder and harder. Oh, my God, I thought, I can't get enough of him.

"Don't stop," I said as he began to thrust faster.

"Oh, God, please don't stop. You feel so good," I said in my state of ecstasy.

I threw my head back, allowing the water to spray me gently in the face. His hands reached down to caress me as he kept up the rhythm in and out of me and I could tell by how I was feeling that I wasn't going to be able to hold on much longer. I was about to explode in ecstasy.

"John, John, I have to…" I tried to tell him but before the words were spoken he whispered in my ear, "Come me with, babe," and as always, we did.

Together.

Our love making didn't stop here. We had an entire night ahead of us, one that would have to sustain us until the next time that we could be together.

Soon after Richie took up residence on the couch we found ourselves inheriting a large sum of money. We decided that it was time to buy a bigger house since we were a family of five and had definitely outgrown our little Cape Cod house. We found a beautiful piece of property in Spring Lake and built a house. It was everything that we had ever wanted: property and within walking distance of the beach.

We moved into our new home when Jonah was just a few months old. I was so hoping that this move would be a new start for Richie and me, wishing that somehow building a new house would help to build a new marriage.

Moving day arrived and the moving company filled our new house with our furniture and box upon box of our belongings. Richie still seemed distant and our bickering was becoming a daily routine, just like cooking and cleaning was.

As I stood in the kitchen, unpacking boxes, I realized that it wasn't just our belongings that I was unpacking. I was unpacking all of our problems right along with my KitchenAid and toaster.

Instead of our boxers being labeled "kitchen" and "bedroom," they should have been labeled "hurt, disappointment, distance and betrayal."

I threw all of my energy into settling into our new home and raising the children. I began to give up on Richie and I, hoping just to survive each day without a major blow up. I kept trying to figure out what had happened to us, where and when it all started going badly, but it was a waste of mindful energy because I couldn't trace it back to any one certain incident or time

We simply existed in our new house together best as we could. Some days were good, some not so good, but we had children to consider and they were always the priority.

At least they were MY priority. They were the first ones to get my attention, my time and my love.

Maybe that was the problem.

Chapter 27

John and I had drifted into a deep sleep on this last night together, locked in each other's arms, as if somehow this would keep us together… and then the phone rang. It was the wake up call, a much different wake up call than I had been giving John the past few mornings.

Room service knocked at the door with the breakfast we had ordered the night before. We ate in silence, both of us keenly aware that we would have to say goodbye in just an hour or so. I started to cry before we even finished our breakfast. John lay his fork down and reached across the table to take my hand into his.

"Please don't cry. This isn't the last time that we'll be together. This is the beginning. You know that. We'll still have our emails, phone calls and texts. Don't worry, I'll try and plan another trip soon. Everything is going to be okay, babe. I promise," he reassured me, kissing the top of my hand.

"I know, I'm just missing you already. I don't want to go home. I've loved being with you for these last few days and it's going to be hard to go home without you. I just wish things…" but he abruptly cut me off.

"Things are the way that they are, no sense wasting time wishing for something different. We know the situation that we're in and that we can't change them, at least for right now. So you stop thinking about the what if's and think about the what is," he said trying to make me feel better

"What is is that we love each other and that we're together forever in whatever way we can be. I love you like no one can and you take that thought with you and hold it in your heart," he said. He smiled at me as he got up to get dressed.

"I know you're right," I said, getting up right behind him. I pulled out my suitcase and laid it on the bed. I threw on my jeans and a t-shirt then proceeded to pack up all of my belongings. It was time to move out of my home, OUR home.

"I have to go down to my room and pack but I'll stop back before I go," John said as he kissed the top of my head. He headed out the door and I continued to pack.

I gave Richie a quick call to tell him that "Colleen" and I would be leaving for the airport soon and that I would call him when I landed. It was a short conversation, it's all that I could handle under the circumstances. I didn't even give him much of a chance to talk, simple and to the point was all I could muster up this morning.

About forty five minutes later John was walking through the door, all dressed for his trip back home, back to his home with Tess. He was trailing his suitcase behind him. He walked over to the bed and asked if I was all packed, then zipped my suitcase for me and placed it on the floor next to his. I checked around the room for any last minute things I may have missed. Nope, I had packed everything, including my memories of this time I had spent with John.

"Okay, my love, it's time to go. Let's say our goodbyes here and head out," he said sadly. It had never occurred to me until this moment that he was hurting as much as I was.

We embraced one another tightly, more tightly than we ever had, as if to hold onto something that we were both afraid to lose. John touched my chin with his finger and brought my face up to look into his eyes. He kissed me, his hands caressing me all over as if he wanted to remember every curve of my body.

We kissed one another for a long time, our tongues touching together, as if to capture the taste of each other to take back home with us on the plane. He pulled away and I knew it was time for us to go.

John took both of our suitcases, pulling one in each hand, and I grabbed my purse off of the bed. We headed out the door, but not before each of us took one more look around at the place that we had made love to each other in for the last three days.

I stepped out into the hallway and heard the door slam shut behind me. We walked onto the elevator together and rode down to the lobby in silence, our teary eyes locked in a gaze with one another. The elevator stopped, the door opened and we stepped out.

We walked to the hotel store to pick up some things for our kids. I grabbed two "Miami" magnets and gave one to John.

"A little something to remember our time," I said.

"Babe, I'll always remember," he said so lovingly that I almost began to cry again.

We walked out into the parking lot and John put my suitcase into the back seat of the Mustang, helping me into the driver's seat.

"Buckle up, don't want anything happening to you," he said.

"I will. God, I'm going to miss this car!" I said as I started the engine and tried to forget what was happening.

"Thanks, babe, glad to know that it's the car that you're going to miss," John joked with me, as if to lighten the somber mood which was now upon us.

"C'mon, now, you know that I'll miss you! I miss you all the time. That's a fact…but I will miss this car!" I joked back with him. He laughed out loud, which made me laugh right along with him.

He bent down to kiss me goodbye again.

Except that this time he was crying.

"Now don't you start crying. You always tell me not to cry. Don't, please, don't. I love you with all my heart and soul, forever and always. Take that home with you," I said, gently wiping away the tear that had fallen down his cheek.

"I know and I love you back the same, even more. I'll call you when I land, or you call me. Oh, whoever lands first calls or texts! Be careful, babe. I don't want anything bad to happen to you. Enjoy the flight and good luck when you get home. Hope the house isn't in too bad of shape," he joked.

"Yeah, right, I'm sure it's a disaster and I'm hoping that it is! The massive clean up will help keep my mind off of missing you," I said, then added "on second thought, NOTHING can take my mind off of you."

We kissed one last time and I drove off, looking in the rear view mirror as John stood there waving goodbye to me.

I got to the airport in a few minutes, returned the car to the rental agency, and took the shuttle to the terminal. It wasn't too long of a wait until boarding time so I grabbed a cup of coffee from the airport Starbucks. The voice on the airline speaker announced that it was time for boarding and with that, I was taking my seat on the plane that was taking me home.

I put on my headphones, turned on my tablet, and settled in for the plane ride home. I was thankful at takeoff that no one was in the seat next to me. I closed my eyes and tried to sleep but instead my thoughts kept drifting back to the last three days that I had just spent with John.

The flight attendant came down the aisle taking cocktail orders. I ordered two glasses of wine, knowing that there would be a car waiting at the airport to take me home.

I drank my wine and listened to my music.

We'd be landing before long and I'd soon be returning to my "other" life.

The wine was making me feel a bit buzzed and I kept thinking "other life?" Or is it "new life?" What life am I living?

It was too much to worry about right now. I had to go home and face a life that would now be changed forever because I was changed.

The plane soon landed, I found my suitcase and just as promised, the limo driver was waiting for me in the terminal with a sign that had my name on it.

"Good trip, ma'am?" he asked.

"Yes, thank you. It was a really good trip," I answered as I got into the back seat of the stretch limo. He put my suitcase in the trunk and we were off. We weren't driving for more than ten minutes when I heard my cell phone ring. I fumbled through my pocketbook to find it and heard the voice that made my heart flutter on the other end.

"Hey, love, it's me. You land okay?" he asked. It was John.

"Yes and I'm guessing that you did as well," I answered, a smile beaming across my face. I'm sure that the limo driver was curious as to who was making me smile like that!

"Sure did. I'm about forty five minutes from home. I'll try and call you tonight, but if Tess is up and about, it's just going to be a text or email. Sound good?" he asked.

"Give her some allergy medication or something so that she goes to bed early," I joked. Tess was notorious for staying up late, making late night phone calls with John near impossible! I often wondered if she knew that something was going on with her husband and stayed up late just to see if she was right.

"Now, now, be nice. I love you and I'll be in touch as soon as I can, okay?" he asked.

"I love you, too. I'll wait to hear from you. Bye," I said and with that, hung up the phone.

Now began the usual routine of an affair.

Of my affair.

Life in our house was getting stranger and stranger with each passing day. Richie was becoming more and more engrossed in different projects, ones that never made much sense to me. To most people it would seem to be normal interests, but he totally immersed himself in his projects, researching them for hours, disappearing after dinner each night to work on them. The kids and I barely saw him but there didn't seem to be anything that we could do to dissuade him.

I had days of feeling overwhelmed at being a mom of three with no help from him, but my time was filled with school, potty training, scouts, sports and church. Richie showed some interest in the different things that the kids did but it always seemed as though it was a bother to him. These things took time away from his projects and he was never happy about that.

Still, life in our house continued. The bickering between Richie and I was becoming less frequent, but so was the talking. We barely spoke to or saw one another. I felt like a single parent, which most days was fine with me. It seemed that the less we saw of each other the better the house ran. The kids were calm and well behaved, acting out on the rare occasion that their father spent time with all of us. Every so often I'd blow up at him and tell him to go back to his projects, back to his "room!" He'd grumble and retreat but I knew he was relieved that I sent him away.

Some days I cried over wondering what went wrong, what happened to us, but with three kids to raise I didn't have time to dwell on it, let alone think about my needs. My needs were simple at this time in my life.

My needs were to just get through the day.

My wants were to have John.

Chapter 28

The limo was turning down my street and I saw the kids on the front lawn exactly where they had been when I left them just three short days ago. As the car pulled up to the house they all ran to the car, screaming for presents.

"What did you bring us?" they yelled with excitement.

"Hugs and kisses first!" I said. I grabbed each and everyone of them and squeezed them, planting kisses on their chubby little cheeks. Richie was walking out of the front door. He came up to me and kissed me, taking my suitcase from me.

"Well, look at you! You made it home safe and sound," he gloated. "See, flying isn't so bad, is it?" he asked.

"Nope, not at all. In fact, consider me a definite flier from now on. I can't wait to fly somewhere else!" I said. I was hoping that where John was concerned it would be soon!

I walked into the house and much to my surprise, found a minimal mess. Richie had actually cleaned and truth be told, I was thankful for that.

I took my suitcase upstairs, unpacked and threw my clothes into the laundry room, but not before taking a deep inhalation of each piece, knowing the scent of John was on each and every one of them.

I hated the thought of washing them, and silly as it may sound, I kept out a t-shirt that had his scent all over it and tucked it under my pillow. At least for tonight, I thought, I need to feel close to him. I need to smell him. It makes the missing a little easier to bear and the feeling of him closer. After all, Richie and I hadn't shared the same bed in years.

The day wore on and it was dinnertime. I was too tired to cook so takeout was the dinner of choice, not to mention an easy cleanup for me. The kids took their baths after dinner and went to bed on time, a concept that Richie didn't seem to adhere to while I was away.

I took my own bath, put on my pajamas and crawled into bed. I made sure that my cell phone was charged and on the nightstand next to me. I was so hoping that John would call and on the nights that he said he'd try to I could never quite fall into a deep sleep.

I went to bed around ten o'clock and fell right to sleep, dreaming of John and I making love. I woke up a few hours later to go to the bathroom and glanced over at the clock. It was one o'clock in the morning. John hadn't called and most likely wouldn't be. The latest he'd ever call was around midnight.

I went to the bathroom and then back to bed. It took me almost two hours to get back to sleep and I soon woke up around six. I jumped out of bed and went straight to my computer to check for an email. There in my inbox was an email from John. I clicked onto it right away.

> Hey, babe, Tess is awake as usual so I can only write you a short note. I have an ache in my heart over missing you and can think of nothing but the last three days and making love to you. Know that I love you and will call you on Monday.
> Forever yours,
> John

Damn her. Now I'd have to wait the entire weekend to hear from him. It's as if she has to watch his every move. Then again, I guess that maybe she does but I hated knowing that SHE was up with John and I wasn't. Well, I had his love, she didn't. I had him body and soul, and she didn't. True enough, I thought, but she's his wife and I'm not. And that was a hard fact for me to deal with.

I threw on my bathrobe and went downstairs to make some coffee. I reached for two of my headache pills and swallowed them down with some water. I don't know why I took them, I didn't have a headache. Actually, I took them to cope with how I felt being without John, of not being his wife, and of missing him so damn much. I took them to survive my life and to cope with dealing with a marriage that I knew in my heart was over.

And that marriage was mine. I only hoped that John was feeling the same.

The day went on as usual and I was glad that I had so much to do. Aside from the normal housework, I had food shopping to do and a lesson plan to write for my Sunday School class in the morning. I was thankful that the time passed by so quickly and that night time had crept upon me. Once again I made sure that my cell phone was next to the bed, just in case John called.

But he didn't call.

And there was no email waiting for me in the morning.

I took two more pills before church and piled the kids into the car. Richie came with us. This was the one thing he insisted on all of us doing as a family. I guess it was better than nothing.

We took the kids to lunch after church, then came home. The kids were outside playing and I decided to take it easy and read. Richie was off in the house busy with one of his projects. I cooked a nice dinner of roast chicken and mashed potatoes, a favorite of the kids, and we all had dinner together. This has become our Sunday tradition. The kids chatted endlessly throughout the meal, stopping once in a while to bicker. Richie ate in silence, barely speaking to any of us. I wondered what was going on in his mind, but didn't waste too much time trying to figure it out. He had become what I called "a man unto himself" and I had given up on working on a marriage that was hopeless.

My life is what it is and I couldn't change it, maybe even "wouldn't" change it at this point. Richie had his good days and his bad, we were just in a stretch of "bad" right now. This had become routine and I knew it would pass in time, at least it had in the past.

The day was nearly over and I got things ready for the Monday morning school rush. School lunches were made, backpacks filled and lined up by the front door, and clothes laid out on the bed. I went to bed exhausted and missing John terribly. I couldn't wait until the morning when he would call me from work.

Here I am again… Waiting.

"Depression. We've tried different medications but they only seem to work for a while. The condition never goes away and can get worse as time goes on." The words from the doctor echoed through my mind in a sort of whirlwind.

And when the wind settled down, I felt as though someone had handed me a life sentence. I left the office and sat in my car, the tears falling lightly at first, turning into sobs that seemed to come from the deepest part of my soul in reaction to all that I had just been told.

It seemed like a lifetime before I was able to start the car and head home.

Home. What kind of home was it becoming? What kind of home had it become?

Richie had kept his depression hidden from me for months. I only found out about it when the doctor called to speak with him. It was when I confronted him about who she was that he finally told me he was suffering from depression.

Here I was, two weeks later outside of the doctors office, now knowing the truth about Richie's change in behavior. My God, what am I going to do? Never mind me suffering from the effects of this disease, but we have three children to consider. I was wishing that someone would just step in and tell me what to do, tell me if there was hope for a full recovery, tell me there was hope for a miracle. But there was no one to tell me those things.

All of this was suddenly dropped onto ME and I had to figure out what to do or if there was anything I could do.

I pulled out of the parking lot and headed home to my children, wondering if I would ever be able to look at Richie in the same way, look at him as my husband. Damn him, why did he have to have this illness?

I was angry at him for being depressed and broken hearted for him in imagining what it must be like for him.

Our lives had changed so much throughout the years and now they were going to change even more and they were going to change forever.

I prayed to God for a miracle, for an answer that I was certain would never come.

It was at that moment that John came into my mind.

He could fix it, or at least try to fix me.

But John was a lifetime ago.

Chapter 29

It was a long and restless night of broken sleep. Jonah had a cold and was tossing and turning all throughout the night. He seemed a bit more perky this morning but still not quite himself. I had barely gotten Billy and Katie on the school bus when the phone rang.

John's calling early, I thought. But when I answered the phone it wasn't John's voice that I heard.

It was Richie's.

"Hey, I hate to start your day off on the wrong foot but I forgot a bunch of papers that I need for work. I can't drive home to get them because I'm getting ready to go into a meeting. Would you please bring them to the office? They're right on my desk," Richie said in a tone less of a question and more of an order.

"Are you kidding me? It's an hour drive there and Jonah is sick. It'll be almost lunch time by the time I get there. I'm not even dressed yet," I complained, knowing that I'd probably run into John and I certainly didn't want him seeing me looking like a disheveled and tired old mommy.

"How's this, if you bring me the papers I'll take you to lunch. See if your mom will stay with Jonah. Please do this for me, it's important. I don't want your old friend, John, thinking that I can't handle this job. I need this job and you need me to keep this job," he said, almost sounding pathetic.

"Fine, I'll bring them up and see you around noon," I said feeling defeated.

"Thanks, I'll make it worth your while because I know that you're so busy all day long," he said sarcastically. "I'll take you to lunch and if you play your cards right maybe a nice night when the kids are asleep," he said with that sickening tone when he wants to have sex. Yes, sex, not making love.

Oh, God, I thought, lunch is plenty, especially since I was just making love to your boss last week.

"Lunch is fine. See you in a little while," and with that I hung up. Great, now I had to rush around and get ready. I called my mom to see if she could watch Jonah. She wasn't thrilled about it since she already had plans of her own, but agreed to do it.

The next step was to wash my hair which didn't thrill me. Mondays were my "at home, grungy, get the house tidied up after the kids have been home all weekend, no hair washing, no makeup" sort of day! So much for those plans!

I threw my head under the kitchen sink and washed my hair. I plopped Jonah down with a popsicle in front of the television while I did my makeup. I threw on my jeans and a t-shirt. I looked in the mirror and decided to change into something a bit more dressy, after all, I was at least hoping for lunch in a somewhat nice restaurant.

Wait, who was I kidding?

I didn't care about dressing nicely for the restaurant. I was dressing nicely for John.

I changed into a pair of black pants, black being my "signature color" and a lightweight white sweater. John always thought I looked cute in white. I even threw on a pair of black, spiked heeled boots.

I looked into the mirror again and smiled. I looked pretty damn good for a mommy of three!

I heard my mom come in through the front door and finished up with my makeup, brushing my hair through one last time and spraying it with enough hairspray to hold it in place through a nor'easter! I barreled down the stairs to see my mom already in the throes of cleaning my house and honestly, I was thankful for that this morning.

"I can't believe he forgot papers. He needs to learn to be more organized!" she complained to me, as if I wasn't already thinking the same.

"I know, but what do you want me to do? I'm not his keeper, just his wife," I snapped back.

"What time will you be back?" she asked, all the while washing dishes in the sink.

"I don't know. It's an hour drive up and back and I guess you can add in about two hours for lunch," I said to her.

"Whatever," she grumbled. Normally her tone would bother me, but not this morning. I was becoming way too excited to worry about it.

I kissed Jonah good-bye, grabbed Richie's papers and got in the car. I stopped for a cup of coffee for the drive and began my hour-long trek up to the office. I was actually glad for the drive.

It was alone time for me, not to mention the fact that I could smoke without worry of the kids catching me. I put on a Fleetwood Mac CD for the drive, playing "Sweet Girl" over and over. It made me think of John who often called me his "sweet girl."

My mind drifted to thoughts of Richie, surprisingly enough, and thinking about how life was going in our house lately.

It wasn't going great but it wasn't going awful.

It was going.

"He's sleeping again?" the kids grumbled. "He's always sleeping. We want to go to the park!"

Richie wouldn't allow me to tell the kids about his depression so I was stuck with the task of trying to cover for him and make excuses for his erratic behavior.

In other words, I had to lie for him.

"Daddy is just tired from working so hard for all of us," I explained. "He'll be up soon."

They always accepted whatever answer, or excuse, that I gave them with a look of disappointment, a look I had seen on their sweet faces far too often these days. After that, they were off in different directions trying to find something else to keep them entertained.

Aside from all of his many projects, which were becoming more and more expensive, Richie took to bed the rest of the time. He'd get up in the morning, take a shower then go back to bed. He gets up around one or two in the afternoon for a short time, then goes back to bed until dinner, where he tries to be awake and around for each night.

He helped put the kids to bed and then would be up all night long. It was a bad pattern that he had fallen into, but for better or worse, this is how life in our house was becoming. I'd try to coax him out of bed with ideas of things to do with the kids or as a family, but he'd always say that he was too tired.

I was becoming a single parent living in a house with a partner, a man, who in my eyes, was giving into this illness without a fight.

I was alone in a house filled with people.

I felt like I was the loneliest girl in the world.

Chapter 30

I followed Richie's directions to the office, having never been there before. It was a large, quite impressive building, very modern looking, set back off the road in a beautiful setting of oak trees. One would never know that it was only minutes off of the New Jersey Turnpike.

I drove down a long road to get to the main parking lot, pulling my car into the lot marked for "visitors." I turned off the engine and took one last look into the mirror, checking my makeup and hair, popping a mint into my mouth. I spritzed myself with the perfume that I kept in the car to hide the cigarette smoke smell from the kids. I grabbed my purse and Richie's papers and walked into the building towards the receptionist.

"I'm here for Richard Burke," I told the woman, no, actually it was more of a young girl behind the desk dressed in a very slinky burgundy dress with way too much makeup and jewelry on.

"Sure," she said between snaps of chewing gum, "I'll let him know that you're here," she said as she called up to his office.

"He's in a meeting right now but someone will be down to take you upstairs to his office," she said, getting back to the magazine she was reading.

"Thank you," I said, waiting nervously for whoever it was that was coming down to take me upstairs.

A few minutes later I heard the sound of the elevator door opening and saw John step out of it. He was dressed in the same black suit and red tie that I had just seen him in last week. He walked towards me, almost sauntered, trying to curtail the wide smile on his face.

"Well hey there, you," he said to me. "Glad you could make the trip all the way up here. What a good little wife you are!" he joked with that sarcastic tone he gets in his voice when he's busting on me.

"Shut up," I joked back. "This is so not fun for me!"

He led me to the elevator and we stepped in. The door had barely closed behind us when he pulled me into his arms and started kissing me feverishly on the lips. His hands were grabbing at my hair and he was rubbing his body up against me.

"Babe, I miss you. You feel great! I'm sorry that I couldn't call. Tess was up all fucking night, as usual, but believe me, that didn't stop me from dreaming about you all night long," he said running his hands down my back and moving around to the spot he knows makes me wet with excitement.

"Stop, John, I'll be all disheveled looking when I see Richie and then what? Do I tell him that his boss attacked me in a moment of passion on the elevator?" I joked, pushing him lightly away from me.

"Yeah, tell him that!" he laughed. "Babe, c'mon, live a little, will 'ya?" he joked back kissing my neck in the spot that he knew could make me get excited.

"I lived a lot last week with you, now behave yourself. I wouldn't want you to get all excited before you have to take me to my husband," I said, this time stepping away from him while fixing my hair and smoothly down my shirt.

"Okay, okay, you're the boss," he said, taking a distinct military step away from me and saluting.

"You are so bad…and then some," I laughed. The elevator doors opened and we walked towards the office door where there was yet another receptionist, this one being a woman in her late 50's, somewhat frumpy.

"Hey, Pat, this is Richie's wife. Think we should let her in?" he said slyly as he gave her a wink.

"Nice to meet you! I just love your husband. He's so sweet," she said to me.

"Take him, he's all yours," I thought to myself.

"Thanks, but are we talking about the same Richie?" I joked with her, but she didn't get the joke and looked at me with a snippy little look, as if I offended her. Obviously Richie was a much happier person at work than he was at home.

I wonder why that was.

Another one of his games?

John and I exchanged a "rolling of the eyes" look at each other, said good-bye to her, and proceeded down a long hallway filled with office doors.

"Richie's still in a meeting so I'll treat you to a cup of coffee in my office," John said, apparently happy that he'd have me all to himself for a little while longer.

He led me down yet another hall to an office door with his name on it. We went into his office, he shut the door, and he locked it.

"You can never be too careful," he said as he took the papers and my purse from me, setting them down on the chair.

"C'mere you," he said, grabbing my hand and pulling me towards him. He wrapped himself around me tightly, grinding his excitement into mine. I couldn't help but reciprocate and we fell into a passionate embrace. I was melting, right here in his office, only doors away from my husband. I couldn't believe what we were doing but I was happy that we were. I wanted to make love to him right there and then and would have if his phone hadn't rang.

I stopped kissing him when I heard the phone but John continued on kissing and groping me. He told me it could wait and that he couldn't. He wanted me now, right there in his office.

The phone kept buzzing and John finally got annoyed enough to answer it.

"Yes?" he asked, quite annoyed.

"She's right here, Richie. Why, are you nervous that I just may have to keep her?" he joked.

"Come on down, we're just sitting here with the coffee and reminiscing about our old high school days."

My heart was racing a mile a minute. This was dangerous and seriously nearing the point of us getting caught which is what I think excited John even more.

Maybe me, too.

I heard a knock at the door and John yelled for Richie to come in, forgetting that he had locked it. I could hear him trying to turn the knob.

"Ooops," John said with a smirk. "Forgot I locked that!"

He got up and unlocked the door, letting Richie in.

"Sorry about that, buddy, seems like everytime that I slam that door it locks itself! I can only imagine what you're thinking!" he joked with Richie who bought that line in a minute.

I, on the other hand, was thinking that John was really pushing the envelope now.

"Hi, hon," Richie said, walking over to me and giving me a kiss on the forehead.

"Hi, here's your papers," I said, grabbing them from John's desk.

"Thanks a lot. I really appreciate it. Now, I promised you a lunch. Want to join us, John?" he asked.

All I kept thinking was "Please say no, please say no, please say no."

"Sure," John answered. "That'd be great! I haven't seen your wife since high school and we can catch up, that is if it doesn't bore you to death," he joked.

"Nope, doesn't bother me. Let's go," Richie said, clearly sucking up to his boss, using me as the middleman in doing so.

"Great, let's go," John said.

Well, this should be interesting, I thought to myself.

I was hoping that Richie was oblivious enough NOT to see the invisible passion and fire between John and I. I was beginning to think that I was in the middle of a bad movie.

How much more bizarre could this situation be?

The three of us headed out of the office, said good-bye to Pat and got into the same elevator that John and I had just been in, doing things that we had no right to be doing.

Things that set my entire being on fire.

John's parents were divorced but we spent every Saturday with his Dad and his wife. I loved being at their house and spending time with them. They treated us as though we were already adults, not the 17 year olds that we really were. We'd hang out in their living room all afternoon and they'd let us have a drink or two while we were there. The drinking age may have been 18 but we were so close to turning 18 that they didn't care.

We'd laugh and talk about anything and everything and then they'd suggest that John and I take a walk before dinner. They lived on a quiet street, no neighbors to bother anyone. John and I walked hand in hand down the street, lightly buzzed from the cocktails we'd been drinking all afternoon. We felt as though we were walking through an enchanted forest.

Once we were out of sight from the house we'd light a cigarette and continue walking together. We didn't usually talk much on these walks, which was typical for us. We always knew what the other was thinking and it was almost as if we had a conversation going on between us through our minds.

John would squeeze my hand now and again, looking over at me, his eyes filled with love for me and only me.

I'd reciprocate with a kiss to his cheek, whispering "I love you" to him, squeezing his hand back. Once we finished our cigarettes we'd head back to the house. The sun was starting to set and there was a slight chill in the air.

"Cold?" he asked.

"A little, it's okay," I answered.

"I'll warm you up, babe," he said as he put his arm around me, pulling me close to him, the two of us just about stepping on one another. We got back to the house just as the sun had set and darkness had settled in.

As we stepped up onto the front porch I grabbed for the doorknob to go inside, but John took my hand, pulled me close and kissed me. This was not just a kiss, but a long, passionate kiss. Our embrace lasted a few minutes before we pulled back from one another, John telling me that he loved me and that he would until the day he died.

And with that said, we walked into the house for dinner.

We ate a delicious roast beef dinner together as a family, laughing and joking with one another, listening to family stories about John when he was younger. I hoped and prayed to be a part of this family sometime in the near future.

Chapter 31

There we were, my husband, my lover and myself all going out to lunch together. All that was missing was Tess. I wondered if things could get any stranger, then again, I knew that they could.

John decided to take his car and as I went to get into the back seat, Richie said, "No, you get in the front. I'll take the back seat."

Richie didn't know that he was already taking a back seat to John.

"Oh, boy," I thought to myself, "I hope I don't reach across the seat to put my hand on John's thigh" which was something I always used to do to him when we were younger and something I still do now. I was conscious of every move I made in this car and would soon be doing the same in the restaurant. I'm thrilled to be seeing John but my anxiety is creeping up on me, worried that this lunch might be the proverbial cat jumping out of the bag.

And I didn't want my husband to find out this way.

We drove to a cute little Italian restaurant only a few minutes from the office. I knew that Richie hated Italian food with a vengeance but when John asked him if this restaurant was okay for him he sucked up and said, "Yeah, I love Italian food!"

I shot him a look that let him know that I knew differently to which he sent me a look back which told me to "shut up!"

Our little threesome proceeded into the restaurant, John holding the door open for Richie and me. We walked in and we were seated at a booth near the back of the restaurant.

"This is my special table here, they know to have it ready for me when I come in," John gloated. Richie smiled as if he was truly impressed and in awe of John.

Once again good 'ol Richie insisted that I sit next to John.

Thanks, pal, I thought to myself. It's bad enough that I can't jump the guy and now I had to practically sit on top of him without showing signs of how much I wanted him.

"Wine, anyone?" John asked knowing full well that I loved my wine!

"No, thanks, I have to drive home after this little lunch," I answered, knowing how wine could make me feel. I certainly didn't want a drop of it in this situation!

"I'll have some if you are, Johnny," Richie answered, once again sucking up to John. And "Johnny?" I'm sure he loved that!

"Great, we'll celebrate your great work at the company and my reunion with your wife! We'll just let her be a party pooper while we have some fun!" John joked, his knee rubbing up against mine under the table.

God, what the hell are you doing? I thought to myself. This was getting a bit out of hand for my liking. I love John but this situation is getting dangerous and I'm beginning to feel very uncomfortable.

Truth be told, I was wishing I was home.

It was no surprise that Richie ordered the same lunch of chicken marsala as John. As for me, just a Caesar salad, if you please.

"Watching your calories?" John busted with me.

"No, just not that hungry," I answered, wanting to slap him at that moment. He knew me well enough to know how uncomfortable this must be for me, yet he kept pushing and pushing, along with pushing his knee harder and harder into mine.

I was thankful that lunch arrived in about fifteen minutes, knowing that this "happy little get together" would soon be over. Then, as if to add insult to this injury, Richie had to speak.

"You know, Johnny, I was thinking that you and Tess should come over to our house for dinner this weekend. This way the girls could get to know each other better," he said. I all but spit out a piece of lettuce across the table. It was at that moment that I grabbed Richie's glass of wine and took a long sip.

"Great idea, we'd love it. Name the date!" John answered. What the hell was he thinking? You stupid ass, I thought, how in the hell would we survive an entire evening together with each other and our spouses?

Ugh, men!

"How about this Saturday? Say about five?" Richie answered without even asking me if this was okay. Now I was beginning to feel like a silent partner.

"Perfect, we'll be there. Should we bring anything?" John said, now rubbing his leg against mine. I was getting too angry to feel excited.

"No, just yourselves! This'll be great!" Richie said excitedly, taking another bite of chicken.

"Um, hello? Guys? Did you forget that I was here?" I asked, quite annoyed. Richie shot me a dirty look across the table, one which said, "Are you out of your fucking mind? That's my boss!"

He kicked my leg slightly under the table and I wondered if he felt John's leg pressed into mine.

"I'm sorry, you're right. Is Saturday okay for you?" John asked, a bit patronizingly.

"Sure, I guess," I said sheepishly, feeling defeated and bullied by both of them. Richie breathed a sigh of relief and you could see the tension drain from his body.

"Good, then we're all set. We'll see you all at five!" he said matter of factly with a tone of "I am the ruler of this roost" in his voice.

Screw you both, I thought.

"Better yet, Richie, I'll leave my kids home. Adults only. Sound like a plan?" John said with an insistent tone in his voice.

Sure, I thought to myself, my husband would kiss your ass any day of the week.

"Sure it's okay," he answered. God, how well do I know this man?

"Great, I'm looking forward to it. Let us at least bring some wine. What do you think you'll be serving?" John asked me.

Your head on a platter, I thought. Yours and Richie's.

"I don't know. We could throw some steaks on the grill," I said, trying to finish my salad as quickly as I could so that this nightmare of a lunch would end. "Filet mignon," Richie added, "Nothing's too good for my boss and his wife!"

Great, honey, just great, I thought.

"Perfect! I'll grab a great bottle or two of wine out of my wine cellar at home. I'm a big collector! We'll have ourselves a real party! Maybe Tess and I will have a car drive us to your place so that we can have a real good time!" John said excitedly.

Really? I thought to myself. Wine cellar? Collector? Who was this John? Not mine because I never knew that about him.

I couldn't help but wonder what in the hell he was thinking, let alone doing. I could tell by the action going on under the table exactly what he was thinking right now, but what was he thinking about this Saturday night?

Jesus, John, seriously? I already hate Tess and now you want me to spend an evening with her.

We were certainly going to have an interesting conversation real soon!

Lunch droned on with the two of them chatting endlessly about work. I kept looking at my cell phone, hoping that one of them would notice me checking the time. I needed to get home, no, I wanted to go home.

An hour and a half passed and we were done with lunch, thank God! John drove us back to the office and I sat in silence staring out of the window for the entire drive. He parked and I leapt out of the car.

"I really gotta go, guys. Thanks for lunch, John, and Richie, I'll see you home. It was very nice to see you again, John," I said as I began to walk to my car.

See you again? I had just seen him last week.

"Wait, you shouldn't walk all the way across this parking lot alone. You never know what could happen," John said looking at me with concern and with lust.

"Oh, sorry, I have a conference call in five minutes," Richie said, looking at the time on his cell.

"That's okay, buddy. I'll make sure that your little wife gets to her car safely and in one piece. You go head up to the office and get ready for your call. Don't want to keep the client waiting," John said looking much too eager for a stroll across a parking lot.

"Great, thanks, Johnny. See you home," Richie said to me with an obligatory kiss to my cheek.

And with that he hurried into the building as John walked me across the parking lot to my car, taking my keys from me and opening the door.

"Are you out of your fucking mind? What the hell are you thinking about us all having dinner together?" I yelled at him.

"Wow, calm down, babe. I'm paving the way for Tess to get to know you and not feel jealous of our friendship. She'll meet Richie, see that you're happily married and won't be suspicious of two old high school sweethearts being friends. It'll do the same for your hubby. Trust me," he said as if he's been master minding this plan for some time.

"You do trust me, don't you, babe?" he said with those puppy dog eyes. He knew that he could make my heart melt every time.

"You may be right but it won't be an easy night, at least not for me. I'm just reeling with excitement at the thought of watching you and your wife all night!" I said sarcastically.

"You know me better than that. You know it won't be that way. You're my sweet girl and nothing can change that. I love you and only you. Tess is just, well, an obligation, let's just say, just as Richie is for you. You and I are real, right?" he asked. Dammit, he always knew the right thing to say to me to calm me down and make me feel safe.

"Alright, I'll trust you on this one, but you better bring more than two bottles of wine because I'm going to need that much to get me through the night," I said, mellowing out a bit and softening my heart towards this man that I loved so much.

"And hey, wine cellar? Wine collector? What's that about?" I asked inquisitively.

"Tess' idea. Didn't want to throw that in your face," he said, almost apologetically.

"Fine, whatever. Let's just get through Saturday night," I conceded.

"That's my sweet girl. It won't be so bad, I promise. Now get home safely and carry my love in your heart with you. Love you, babe," he said as he took my hand, looked around to be sure there was no one in the parking lot watching us, and kissed the top of it. I kissed the top of his hand back and watched him as he walked across the lot and into the building.

I got in the car and started the engine.

I was glad that it was an hour drive home.

John and I barely fought but every once in a while he'd do something that would really piss me off. It was a week before the neighboring Catholic school prom when John told me that he was taking a girl from work to it.

"Listen, her boyfriend just dumped her and she's spent a lot of money on her dress. She asked if I'd take her, just as friends," he said defensively.

"Bullshit! She's had her eye on you for a long time and suddenly, you decide to take her to the prom because her boyfriend dumped her and you feel pity for her! You expect me to understand that? Maybe I should do the same thing to you and see how you like it!" I yelled at him.

"Come on! Don't make more out of this than it is. Are you that insecure about our relationship? You're acting like a jealous girlfriend!" he yelled back.

"Fuck you, John. Fuck you. You can be such an asshole sometimes!" I yelled as I walked away from him. He grabbed me by my arm to stop me.

"Dammit, I love you and only you. I'm just helping out a friend from work. Do you want to come with us?" he asked, trying any tactic he could to soften me up.

"Whatever, John, you go and have a great night with her but I can't promise that I won't find something else to do that night," I said in an almost threatening tone.

"What the fuck does that mean? Another guy?" he said angrily. I guess "my tactic" on him was beginning to work.

"It means that if you can go to a prom, of all things, with another girl who you say is just a friend, then I can do the same. That's fair, don't you think?" I asked him hoping that he would say that he wouldn't go after all.

"You know what? That would be okay with me," he answered and it was not the answer I had hoped for. My tactic had backfired right into my face.

I told him to leave me alone and I walked into my parents house. I could hear the squeal of the tires as he pulled out of the driveway.

When he came to pick me up for school the next morning, I wasn't home. I had taken the bus.

I managed to dodge John most of the day at school and decided to take the bus home. As the bus was starting to leave the parking lot I could see John standing by his car, waiting for me to come out of the school so that he could drive me home.

He didn't stop over after school and didn't call that night, but I was too angry to be scared.

We didn't speak for most of the week and before I knew it the night of the prom was here. I tried to get Colleen to go out but she had a date. It was bad enough that my boyfriend would be out dancing with someone else all night, now I'd be home alone all night with nothing to do except think about it.

Life really sucked right about now.

It was near ten o'clock when I decided to give up and go to bed. I put my pajamas on and went upstairs, only to hear my Dad yell up that John was here. It was too early for the prom to be over, so I couldn't imagine what he was doing here. I dragged myself down the stairs to find him standing at the bottom, dressed in a black tuxedo.

"Throw on some clothes. Your dad said that I can take you out for an hour," he said firmly to me. I didn't answer him but went back upstairs to throw on jeans and a hoodie. I wasn't in the mood to worry about putting makeup on.

I came downstairs only to find John pacing back and forth at the front door. He looked into my eyes.

"Let's go," he said with no emotion in his voice.

This is it, I thought, it's the break up coming.

I left the house with him and got into the car, staying on my side. Usually I would slide into the middle to cuddle with him while he was driving.

John drove us down to the Manasquan Inlet and parked the car. He got out and opened the door for me then told me to face the inlet while he got something out of the car. As I watched the lights shimmering across the Inlet I heard him open the trunk of his car.

Within a minute I heard Peter Frampton's song, "Baby I Love Your Way," playing through the car speakers, filling the air with the sounds of music. He walked around to face me, a wrist corsage in hand. He placed it on my wrist, pulled me into his arms and began to slow dance with me, right in the street.

"You're the only prom date that I ever want," he said as we danced and danced and danced.

Chapter 32

I cleaned the house for an entire week, making sure that all the PlayDoh was scraped off of the floor and the popsicle stains on the couch were cleaned off. I washed all of the little handprints from the windows and television screen.

The house was looking pretty good. Richie was pleased with how everything looked and even showed signs of being his old self. He couldn't show the "depressed Richie" side to his boss. I wished that he had thought as much of the kids and me as to hide that side from us as well.

C'est la vie.

Saturday was here and it was the day of the "Dreaded Dinner Party," as I had dubbed it. My mom was going to pick the kids up for a sleepover but not until after John and Tess arrived.

Richie picked up filet mignon and I began baking potatoes, steaming asparagus and making Hollandaise sauce. I was also making marinated tomatoes and onions like we used to have at John's parents house back in high school. I wondered if he would remember.

Richie was dressed in khaki pants and a brown polo shirt. I have to say that he actually looked pretty cute. I opted for black khaki cropped pants and a white v-neck shirt along with a pair of black sandals.

I heard the doorbell ring from my bedroom and heard Richie yelling, "They're here!"

I ran down the stairs just as he was opening the front door. There they stood, John and his wife, Tess. I was staring at the woman whose shoes I wish I was in.

John was dressed in light colored pants and a black polo, a color that accented his gray colored hair. Tess was wearing a floral skirt and short sleeved sweater. She definitely wasn't what I had expected. I guess I had thought that she'd look like I used to, a slightly overweight, frumpy housewife with nothing more to her wardrobe than sensible "mommy" clothes.

Surprise! What I saw standing before me was a woman that was younger than me with long, dark hair, slim and definitely in shape, wearing "sexy" clothes.

And she was pretty. Almost beautiful. Her smile lit up her face. She wasn't wearing much makeup, but then again, she didn't need to.

"Hey, guys, this is my wife, Tess," John said as he led Tess through our front door, guiding her with his hand which was placed on the small of her back.

"Hi," she said, "it's so nice of you to have us for dinner on such short notice. You're quite a good sport! If John had dropped this one on me I would have killed him!" she joked to me, shaking my hand.

"No worries. It isn't any trouble at all," I said as I lied through my teeth. I had barely spent any time with my kids all week while I was preparing for this night.

Richie led everyone out onto the back deck where a pitcher of iced tea and wine glasses were waiting alongside a tray of fresh veggies and various cheeses.

True to his word, John was carrying three bottles of wine. He opened the first one immediately and poured all of us a glass. Then, as if that weren't enough, the idiot toasted us to "a newfound friendship!" God, this man was something else and at that moment I wasn't sure what!

We all sat down together on the deck and began to chat. I struck up a conversation about parenting with Tess. Other than both of us being in love with her husband it seemed to be the only thing that we had in common.

Richie put the steaks on the grill and I excused myself so that I could check on the rest of dinner. I was sure to bring my glass of wine with me.

"Why don't I go in and give your wife a hand?" John asked. "You two seem to be deep in conversation and I hate to leave her with all the work while we're all out here having a good time without her."

"She's fine, John, you don't have to help her," Richie insisted.

"Let him go, Richie," Tess interrupted, "it's not fair that your wife is stuck inside doing all the work and John promised ME a relaxing night. This will be his good deed for today. Besides, you and I can have a good time without them," Tess joked.

"Alright then, buddy, go and do your duty! I'll keep Tess company for you," he said and with that he refilled Tess' glass with wine and continued their conversation about the work that John and he do at the company.

John grabbed his wine along with the half empty bottle from the table and headed inside to the kitchen.

"Gotta keep the girls drinking at the same pace! Your wife probably needs a refill, too," John said as he walked into the house. He must have read my mind as I had just downed the last sip of wine in my glass.

I heard the door open and saw John pop his head in.

"I heard that someone needs a refill!" he said, holding up the half empty bottle of wine and walking in. He closed the door behind him and walked towards me. My hands were in a sink of soapy water, washing the pot that I had cooked the asparagus in.

"You read my mind! My glass is on the table," I said as I motioned to it with my head, my hands still in the sink. John walked over to fill my glass I went back to washing the pot when I felt his warm body come up behind me, pressing himself into me. He wrapped his arms around my waist and began to kiss my neck. I let my head fall back onto his shoulder just as I was letting myself fall back into the moment.

"John," I started to say but before I could finish my sentence he pressed his mouth over mine with a long, wet French kiss. I slipped my tongue into his mouth as I was beginning to feel a small effect from drinking the first glass of wine so quickly and on an empty stomach.

"Mom, we're leaving soon," Katie yelled on her way into the kitchen. John quickly stepped back and reality slapped the small buzz right out of me.

My God, I thought, did she see anything?

"Well hello there, young lady. You must be Katie," John said while trying to cover the moment that had just happened.

"Hi," she said politely but with a tone of "what are you doing alone with my mom?"

"Not staying for dinner?" John asked.

"No, we're all leaving to go to my grandparents for the night," she said with an angry tone in her voice. She shot me a dirty look and I wasn't sure if it was the normal look of a twelve year old girl or if she had seen her father's boss pressed into the back of her mother.

"Mom," she said as if she were trying to snap me back into reality. "We're leaving!"

"Okay, sweetie, have a good time and I'll pick you all up in the morning," I said as I dried off my soapy hands and walked towards her to give her a kiss goodbye.

The boys were darting down the stairs and into the kitchen.

"See 'ya!" they yelled at me as they ran out the front door.

"Nice to have met you, Katie," John said.

"Nice to meet you, too," she said with a polite, yet cold tone in her voice. Within seconds she was out the door and in my mom's car. I heard them pull out of the driveway.

"Do you think she saw anything?" I asked John as he handed me my glass of wine.

"You worry too much, babe. Drink this and you'll feel better. Lighten up, everything is fine," John said as he took a sip of his wine. He led me out through the door to join the others, his hand on the small of my back, guiding me outside, just as he had done with Tess when they arrived.

My mind couldn't stop thinking about Katie walking in on us. She'd been pretty sassy lately so this could possibly be just another one of those moods. I certainly hoped that's what this was.

The wine was kicking in and I was starting to feel much more relaxed. I wasn't worrying anymore about Katie. I'm sure that she didn't see a thing…

At least I hoped that she didn't.

Atlantic City here we come! I couldn't believe that we were going! John and Colleen's boyfriend, Frank, had come up with the idea for all of us to go to Zaberer's Restaurant in Atlantic City then to Harrah's Casino afterwards. Colleen and I were so excited to go! We had never been there before and couldn't wait!

We went to the mall the week before to shop for the perfect outfits and found what we believed to be the perfect attire for a night in Atlantic City,

It was Saturday and John showed up around two in the afternoon to pick me up. He was wearing a dark, navy blue suit with a red and blue striped tie. He looked so handsome! I had on a burgundy colored dress and had spent a good portion of the morning on my hair, makeup and nails. He showed up with a bouquet of carnations, my favorite, took one out, broke off the stem and placed it over my ear in my hair.

"Beautiful," he said.

"As long as YOU think so," I said, checking one last time in the mirror to see how I looked with the flower in my hair. No adjustments necessary. He knew just how to place it in my hair.

"I always think you're beautiful, even on the days you call your yucky days," he joked. "Let's stop by my dads before we go. They're anxious to see us all dressed up in something other than jeans and a hoodie!"

"Great! I love your family. Let's go," I said, grabbing a white wrap that I had bought to complete the ensemble.

John helped me into the car and we were off to his dad's house. When we got there they were waiting for us with camera in hand and a cocktail for each of us on the kitchen counter.

"Have a quick drink before you go. They're not too strong and then we'll take some pictures. You two look great, just like a newly married couple," his dad said. His dream was for John and I to be married one day. It was my dream, too.

We drank cocktails quickly and posed in the front yard for a few pictures. They kissed us goodbye and I noticed John's dad slipping some money into his hand. John nodded at his dad and they hugged one another. It was a sweet picture all of its own.

Now we were off to pick up Colleen and Frank.

Frank was already at her house when we got there and there were more pictures to be taken by Colleen's parents. The four of us got into the car and headed for the Garden State Parkway.

John turned on some music, Southern rock, of course and he and Frank shared a joint while we were driving. It took us only about two hours to get to the restaurant where our table was waiting for us.

We sat down and ordered drinks. Pina Coladas for Colleen and I and beer for the boys. A woman in black pants and a crisp, white shirt came by our table with a camera. She was the resident photographer of the restaurant and asked if we would like a souvenir photo of our evening.

"Sure would," John said.

And with that she snapped a few pictures of the four of us. So young, so happy and carefree and so in love.

By the time we ordered dessert the picture was ready for us. It was a black and white and I couldn't help but notice just how much alike that John and I looked. We had the same color hair, same smile and same eyes. They say that the longer a couple is married the more that they begin to look alike. Maybe John and I were like that already. We finished up our dinner and drove over to the casino.

The four of us were amateurs at gambling and didn't have the luxury to lose a lot of money so we stuck to the slot machines. Colleen and Frank walked away with about $100 and John and I about $75.

But we didn't care. We were two couples out on the town and having a great time!

We were all a little drunk and still in a party mood. The casino had a disco in it so the four of us headed in for some dancing. I think we invented the phrase "dance the night away" because we did just that until a little after midnight when we decided to head home.

We dropped Colleen and Frank off at her parents house and took off on our own. I thought that John was taking me home but instead he drove to "The Pits," as we called them, a very secluded wooded area that we would *frequently go to and drink beer and make love. It was the spot that everyone in our high school used for that!*

We had already been drinking and now it was time to "make love." We pulled into "our spot" and turned off the engine. John grabbed a blanket out of the trunk and we hopped into the back seat.

John was on top of me almost immediately, his hands grabbing at my breasts under my shirt. He ripped off his shirt, then his pants and boxers. I made sure that the blanket stayed draped over him to keep him warm, although I knew that in a short while he'd be more than warm, he'd be hot!

He lifted off my top, slid down my stockings and panties and unhooked my bra. He moved his hand from my breasts to between my legs, making me wet with his touch. I began to squirm with excitement which became his cue that I was ready for him.

He spread my legs apart with his hand while planting passionate kisses on my lips. His body slid into place over mine and the next thing I knew, he was inside of me, deep inside of me, loving me with every ounce of his being. I wrapped my legs around him and we found our rhythm together. I loved the feeling of him thrusting deep inside of me and became excited with each one until I was just about ready to release all the passion from my body.

Our lovemaking lasted longer than usual, a nice surprise for both of us. Soon our excitement built to the point of no return and his love filled all of me and my passion exploded all over him.

The car windows were completely steamed up as he still lay on top of me. He kissed me gently all over my face, expressing his love for me with his eyes. I cupped his face in my hands, looked him in the eye and said "I love you so much that it scares me. I've never felt like this before. I want us to be together forever, John."

"Now don't you spend your time being scared. We're going to be together for eternity and even after that! I promise you that. I'll never, ever leave you," he reassured me.

We must have fallen asleep because it was the early morning sunlight that woke me up. John was laying half on top of me and half on the side of me. I kissed him and nudged him to wake up. He was groggy as he found his way out of a deliciously deep sleep.

"You've got to get me home, babe," I whispered in his ear.

"*I know. I just wish that we could wake up together every morning of every day, just like this,*" he said as we both sat up and began to put our clothes back on.

We hopped into the front seat and were on our way back to my house.

The evening was perfect, from start to finish.

Then again, every moment that I spend with John is perfect...

Every single moment.

Chapter 33

"John, you have to be careful. I think my daughter saw us, seriously, I do," I said with concern.

"Babe, it's fine. She didn't see anything," he tried to reassure me.

But something inside of me told me otherwise.

John and I finished our wine quickly while standing in the kitchen and thank God, dinner was ready. This "dreaded dinner party" wouldn't go on much longer.

At least I had hoped it wouldn't.

"Okay, John, my part of the dinner is ready. Enough with your shenanigans in here. You're playing with fire and you're throwing me right into the flame!" I said, feeling a bit annoyed.

"I'll check with Richie about the steaks. I hope to God they're done!" I said.

"You worry too much. I'll grab Tess and Richie and see you in the dining room," he answered.

John walked outside to tell them that dinner was ready and I put all the food on the table. Richie followed Tess and John in with a platter of steak. I couldn't wait for this night to be over.

The four of us sat down to dinner, one that was actually quite delicious, I might add. John continued filling everyone's glasses with wine the minute he saw that they were empty. I was so afraid that the wine would bring out the truth about John and I and I'm sure that Tess and Richie weren't ready for that.

I know I wasn't.

The four of us ate and made small talk. Actually, Richie and Tess did most of the talking.

"Sometimes I wonder what John does on these business trips!" Tess said. She was a bit drunk and it was showing.

"I do business on my business trips, Tess," John answered sternly.

"I want to go on a business trip!" Richie added. "My wife can get away for her little girls trips but I can't get a business trip!"

"I'll see what I can do about that," John answered with a tone in his voice and look on his face that said that he'd had enough of this night as well.

We finished dinner, had some chocolate mousse for dessert and the party was over.

Thank God!

"Thanks for having us," Tess said. "You'll have to come to our house next!"

"That would be lovely," I answered, wanting to throw up the dinner I had just eaten. There's no way in hell I'm going to their house or having them over again.

We said our "good nights" and they were gone.

I was so glad that the dinner party had ended by ten. John and Tess had to get home to their kids and to pay the sitter. And truth be told, I was thankful for that.

Once they left Richie went on and on about how great the night was and what a great wife John had. Blah, blah, blah! I really didn't care about how great his wife was. My mind was wondering that if she was so great then why was John with me?

"That went great, hon," Richie said.

"I'm glad you think so," I answered and with that I threw the dishes into the sink and headed upstairs to go to bed.

I could have smacked John for this little charade of a dinner party. But instead I fell asleep to dreams of making love to him.

"Hey, a lot of the gang from school are going to the Red Ranch tonight, kind of a last get together. Wanna go?" John asked when he called me.

"Sure, are Colleen and Frank going?" I asked.

"They sure are. I already talked to Frank. I'll be over in an hour to get you! This is going to be awesome!" John said excitedly.

I called Colleen just to be sure she was okay with the plans and she was.

We loved the Red Ranch. It sat on the Manasquan River with a beautiful view of the water and the boats coming in and out. Many of our high school teachers went there so it'd be nice to see them one last time.

John showed up within an hour and I ran out to the car. I hopped in and slid across the bench seat of our beloved car, "Rosie."

"I love this car, John, we've got a lot of good memories in her!" I said in a sexy tone of voice.

"You bet we do and many more to come, literally, sweet girl!" he joked back.

We arrived at the Red Ranch and it looked as though half of our high school class was there already. This was going to be an awesome night!

Colleen and Frank were in the parking lot waiting for us. We walked over to them and John lit a joint for us to share. As we passed it between us we talked about how our "packing for college" was going and that we couldn't believe that next week we'd all be leaving.

I didn't want to think of leaving John and I especially didn't want to think about it tonight.

The four of us walked inside and it looked as though our high school class had rented the place and taken it over. There was live music, lots of drinks going around, and a strong smell of weed!

We partied, we danced and we said our goodbyes to the classmates we weren't going to see for some time.

It was near 2 in the morning when the bar started flashing its lights to let us know that it was "last call."

It was time to go home.

And I was ready to do just that.

But I wasn't ready to say goodbye to my John.

Chapter 34

We skipped church on Sunday and I decided to dive into the massive pile of laundry that was waiting for me. As I was passing by Billy's room I could hear Katie talking with him. I stood to the side of the door to listen in without them knowing.

"You're crazy," Billy said.

"I know what I saw. Dad's boss was practically standing against Mom's back. Is that so innocent like you say?" she said adamantly.

"Katie, it's Dad's boss and Mom's old friend," he tried to reassure her.

"Old BOYFRIEND!" she interrupted.

"Whatever. Mom would never be that stupid. The guy was probably just standing close to talk to her. And so what if he did hug her or something? They KNOW each other and friends hug each other. You're such a baby sometimes, now get out," Billy said, obviously annoyed at his little sister.

I had to wonder if he was annoyed at her for being wrong or at knowing that she was right and felt as though he had to cover for me.

"You're a baby, too!" Katie indignantly said to her brother. I heard her start to leave so I pretended to just now be walking down the hall with a laundry basket.

"You okay, Katie?" I asked her.

"Fine," she answered as she walked into her room and slammed the door.

Dammit, she did see something, I thought to myself. I just wish I knew how much she saw.

I needed to talk to John soon. I sent him an email and told him about the conversation between Billy and Katie, but I didn't get a response.

Five days had passed since the dinner party and I hadn't heard one word from John by phone, email or text. Something was up, something was wrong, I could feel it. I could always feel when something was amiss with John and I knew that my instincts were right this time, too.

My stomach felt uneasy and my heart was hurting. I think I knew what he was thinking and feeling and I think I knew what was about to happen.

A week after the dinner party I finally received an email from John. And it said:

Hi, sorry that I haven't been in touch. I needed time to think about things.

Firstly, you must believe that I love you but I can't play this game anymore. It's not fair to you, to me or Richie or Tess. I owe it to my family to work things out.

I need to help Tess grow into a different person so that our marriage is better. Sorry about this decision that I've made but my mind is made up. I'm sure that you can understand.

Since I've made this decision I feel as though a giant weight has been lifted from my shoulders and I feel more like myself now than I have been for the last few months.

I'm happy and feel more in control of my life. I'm a better person for it.

I'm sure that I've hurt you, I understand that, but you need to get over it.

I hope that we can still be friends. If you want me to call you I will but I cannot continue having a relationship with you other than friendship.

In time you'll see that this is the right thing for both of us.

John

I sat there in front of my computer screen, feeling stupefied as I kept reading his email over and over again. I knew it, I just knew it. Damn him. How could he make such a decision about our relationship without even discussing it with me? Didn't I have an opinion or a say in how I felt? Wasn't I a part of this relationship? Wasn't I just as important as he was?

Suddenly the pain hit, my heart broke and I felt so alone and lost. I needed to get out of the house right away so I ran down to tell Richie that I was going out for coffee.

I got into the car and headed down to the beach where I found a quiet spot to park and cry. And cry, and cry, and cry. I felt like the floor had fallen out from under me and I was terrified. I didn't know what to do.

I reached into my purse and grabbed my cell phone to call John.

I didn't hear John's voice on the other end but a recorded message that said he was no longer taking calls.

He blocked me from his phone.

After about an hour I headed home, feeling hurt and pretty damn mad. I went into the house and straight up to my computer to answer his email.

You bastard! How dare you end this relationship without discussing it with me! You're a fool to think that you can change Tess to "fit your marriage." Good luck trying. It'll never happen.

Thanks for letting me know just how bad being with me made you feel. You broke my heart and I'll never forgive you for that.

And I did try to call you but you blocked me from your phone.

Go to hell and don't ever speak to me again.

"Me"

I hit "send" and within seconds the email was kicked back. He blocked me from that, too.

I went downstairs to fix dinner, my life in a state of suspended animation.

The true love of my life was gone yet again.

He blocked me from his life.

It was the day I was to leave for college. My parents and John were going to drive me there. The car was packed with what seemed like everything that I owned. John and I snuggled into the back seat, his arm wrapped around me more tightly than he ever had before.

It was a four hour drive to the school which would be our last four hours together until Thanksgiving break. No one really spoke much, merely idle conversation. My parents were sad, too. I was their first born and the first to leave the nest.

John and I talked throughout the drive, making plans for the next time we would see each other. We didn't want to wait until Thanksgiving so we were trying to figure out how and when we could make that happen. We talked about him coming down to my school one weekend and me going to his the next.

We talked about our nights on the beach, our trip to Atlantic City, the prom, our high school classes, everything.

We spoke in whispers so that my parents wouldn't hear too much of our intimate details. We kissed a bit and held each other's hands for the entire four hour drive.

Soon signs for the college started to appear on the roadside and we all knew that the inevitable moment of goodbye was getting closer and closer by the minute.

My Dad found a parking spot near my dorm, the place that would be my "home" until June! The four of us made several trips up and down the stairs to the second floor of Carpenter Hall until the last box was brought up. My Mom kept herself busy by making up my bed and unpacking my clothes. John unloaded the boxes of our pictures and mementos of times we had spent together.

I had an "I LOVE YOU" coffee mug, a dried out prom corsage, records from John's personal collection, to name a few. I could see that he was fighting back tears as he set up our pictures on my desk and dresser.

Everything was done and there was nothing left to do now except to say "goodbye." We all walked out to the car. My Dad hugged me goodbye first, handing me fifty dollars "just in case you need it." My Mom started to cry as she hugged me, giving me a last minute piece of advice of "you be careful and watch out for yourself." They both got into the car to allow John and I a few last moments together in private.

We hugged one another and John started to cry, really cry hard.

"What am I going to do without you? I can't stand the thought of being apart from you! You're my whole life and I don't feel like a whole person with you. What am I going to do?" he cried as if I had just broken his heart.

But both of our hearts were breaking over being apart.

Now I was crying.

"John, you'll be fine, I'll be fine. We'll both be fine. We love each other and twelve or so hours of distance between us won't change that. I'll never leave you, ever. Please don't be so sad. My heart is breaking over leaving you," I cried as I buried my head into his shoulder.

"Please, don't leave me, I love you so much, please don't leave me," he pleaded. His crying was getting and my shirt was wet with his tears where his head was buried into my shoulder.

"I won't leave you, promise. Promise," I said, wiping the tears from his eyes and mine.

My Dad yelled out that it was time to go. My Mom got out of the car to console John and get him into the car.

"Come on, John, it'll be okay. You two can talk on the phone tonight when we get home. Don't cry, it'll all be alright," she said, trying to make him feel better.

"I know," he said to her, "I just love her so much and my heart is breaking."

"I know, John, but we have a long drive home and she has to settle in. Let's go, please," my mother pleaded with him as she got back into the car.

John and I kissed one more time, a kiss that seemed to last a lifetime, a kiss that would have to sustain us for months. Our bodies separated and he got back into the back seat of the car, still crying.

John rolled down the car window and stuck his head out. As my father slowly pulled away John yelled out "I love you…forever! What am I going to do without you?"

I waved back and blew him a kiss. I watched as the car pulled away and wondered what he would do without me.

Time would eventually let me know just what he would do and did do without me.

Drinking and drugs.

Chapter 35

A month has passed since I responded to John's email and had been blocked on his phone. I hadn't heard a word from him. Aside from his name being mentioned by Richie once in a while I tried not to think of him. But I did, all the time.

The hurt was still there and I wanted so badly to call him and hear his voice, but I couldn't, knowing that he had blocked me from every facet of his life. I'm surprised that he hadn't fired Richie by now. That way he could have wiped out any and all memories of me.

There were days that I thought that maybe John was right. Maybe ending our relationship was the right thing to do. His email let me know just how badly I made him feel and I loved him too much to do that to him.

Yet didn't he love me enough not to make me feel bad?

Obviously not.

I tried my hardest to hate him for what he did. At least if I could hate him it would make getting over him easier. There were so many reasons to hate him yet there was only one reason why I couldn't.

I loved him.

Hate would have been easy but impossible because no matter how much pain he was causing me, I still loved him in spite of it. I love him just as much now as I always did.

Maybe even more.

I tried to make the best of things, even trying to turn a bad marriage with Richie into a better one. He had his good days and bad, but no matter what I tried, nothing seemed to bring him closer to me and the kids. We made love once but through it all I could only see John in my mind's eye. I felt as though I was cheating on John!

Richie and I haven't made love since and I don't think he even cares.

I wish that I had been the one to leave John, wish I had been the one who had "come to my senses." Right now there's a piece of me that wishes that I could hurt him as badly as he hurt me. He deserves to feel the pain that he inflicted on me. He needs to know just how it feels.

The kids weren't due home for another hour and Jonah was napping, home yet again with another cold. I grabbed a glass of iced tea and went upstairs to check my emails, not that there was anything of importance there, just a few random emails from my girlfriends.

I logged on and looked at my inbox. My heart jumped when I saw one from John, the subject line saying "I'm sorry." I hit the key to open up the email and see what he had to say.

My sweet girl,

How can I begin to say that I'm sorry for ending things? How can I begin to tell you that I was wrong? Do I even have the right to ask you to forgive me?

You were right about changing Tess and I was wrong to say that I was better without you. I'm not better without you. I'm miserable and hurting. There's an ache in my heart in wanting to be with you.

I want to hold you again, kiss away the hurt that I caused you and make love to you forever.

Can you forgive me?

Please say that you can because I don't think that I can live without you. I love you and I've not stopped.

Forgive me, my love.

I need you.

John

Once again I found myself sitting and staring at the screen, reading over and over again his words of apology and confessions of love. My heart jumped at the thought of him wanting me back, while at the same time I couldn't forget what he had done and what he put me through.

I logged off of my computer and went outside to sit on the deck. My mind wandered back to Miami, remembering how it felt to be in his arms, remembering the touch of his hands all over my body, remembering how happy, loved and safe I felt.

I wanted all of that again.

I wanted my sweet boy back and I loved him enough to forget what he had done.

I went back upstairs to my computer and read his email one more time, thinking about what my response would be.

And then I prepared myself to jump… yet again.

The first two weeks at college had been terrible. I missed John so much that I couldn't stand it and he felt the same. I decided to take a bus down to his school in Virginia. The ticket was $50 which was all the money that my father had given to me the day he brought me to school.

I cut class on Friday, bought my ticket and boarded the Trailways Bus bound for The University of Virginia. I was afraid to tell my parents that I was going because they would have told me that I couldn't go, although that wouldn't have stopped me. It was the first time that I traveled alone, and on a bus, and I was scared to death, but knowing that John would be waiting for me made the fear worth it.

The bus ride took forever, stopping at The Maryland House for a break. It was after dinner and still another hour or two before I reached John. An old woman sat down next to me on the bus for the rest of the trip and feeling safe next to her I was able to close my eyes and sleep until we arrived in Virginia.

I awoke to her gently tapping my arm to tell me that we were in the bus terminal. It took me mere seconds to come out of my sleep, grab my bag and run off the bus.

And run I did right into John's arms. He had been waiting outside of the bus door for me.

We both started to cry but didn't want to waste what precious little time we had by standing at the bus so we hopped in the car and were off to his dorm room.

His roommate had graciously agreed to stay out for the weekend, leaving us all alone in their room. We made love until we fell asleep with exhaustion.

The next day it rained, keeping us inside the dorm. We spent the entire day wrapped in each other's arms. John played music as we clung desperately to one another, knowing that my bus would be leaving early the next morning to take me back to school.

To take me away from him.

I was starting to feel sick. I didn't know if I was catching the flu or if it was simply from having to leave him again.

The day went by so fast - a cruel trick of life in knowing that we only had so much time together. We ate dinner in John's room and made love for most of the night, in the hopes that it would sustain us until we were together again. A deep sleep descended upon us late that night, keeping us in the same position we had fallen asleep in until we awoke in the morning to the sound of the alarm clock.

It was time to leave.

We dressed, I packed and we drove in silence to meet the bus. John bought me a large cup of coffee and a muffin for the ride.

The bus was waiting at the terminal when we got there, just about ready to leave. Good thing, too. I don't think that either of us could have tolerated too long of a goodbye. We hugged and kissed and I got on the bus, feeling worse than ever.

I found a seat by the window and waved to John. He blew me a kiss, put his hand over his heart and threw it back to me. It was our way of saying "take my heart with you." The bus pulled away and our eyes remained fixed upon one another until we were out of each other's sight.

I settled back into my seat and fell asleep.

The bus arrived back at my school after midnight and by then I knew that I was sick. My entire body ached, I felt cold and had chills. I walked back to my dorm but had to wait almost a half hour for the security guard to come by and let me in and by then I could barely stand up.

He unlocked the door and I found my way up to my dorm where I plopped down into the bed, my clothes still on. I kicked my shoes off and pulled the blanket over me. I was definitely sick.

I awoke in the morning with a high fever. John had called but I was too sick to get out of bed and walk down the hallway to the pay phone. My roommate took the call for me and assured him that I'd be fine and that I loved him.

After a few days of antibiotics I felt better, but still very weak. I was able to call John and we talked for almost an hour. The pain in missing him was becoming unbearable and I didn't know how much more I could take…and neither did he.

I was beginning to notice from our phone calls that John was drinking more than usual and getting high every day. I expressed my concerns to him about this but he assured me it wasn't a problem.

"It's college," he would always respond.

I knew it was his way of making the unbearable bearable.

A month flew by and this time it was John's turn to visit. He drove Rosie down to my school and we pooled our money together to check into a cheap hotel room where we spent two wonderful nights together.

We made love endlessly until the morning that he had to leave. Once again we were faced with the pain of leaving one another.

I was beginning to wonder just how much longer we could keep doing this…

Chapter 36

I sat down at the computer and began to type…

I hardly know what to say or where to begin. Your email came as a complete surprise to me, albeit a welcome one.

Of course I can forgive you but I can't forget, and I can't help wondering that if we do get back together that you won't do this again to me. I can't take that again. The hurt was terrible and I feel as though I've been nothing more than an invisible person to my family for the last month or so.

Having said all that, yes, I'll jump right back in again. I love you, plain and simple. I'm glad that you came to your senses about Tess. She may be your wife but I'm your true love and your soulmate. She'll never have that.

I'm yours now and forever.

The ball is in your court.

I'll wait until you make the next move and we'll take it from there.

I love you.

"Me"

I hit "send" and went about my day with a spring in my step and a heart that was soaring. The kids were rushing in through the front door when the phone rang. It was John. I headed upstairs so that I could talk to him privately.

"Thank you, thank you, thank you for giving me another chance! I was such a fucking fool to end things with you and I promise that

I'll never do that again to you, ever. I love you so much and I've been miserable without you," he said like a desperate man who had just been given a second chance, a LAST chance.

"It killed me to see Richie at work. Just hearing him mention your name brought an ache to my heart. I'd sneak into his office while he was out just to look at your picture," John said without taking a breath.

"Don't keep thanking me, love. I love you. Let's put it behind us and move on.

For God's sake, John, we've been together for almost a year now without either of our spouses knowing what's been going on. It's time to plan a celebration, a sort of "reconciliation celebration! What do you think?" I asked with a happiness in my voice that I hadn't had since he left me.

"Perfect! You're right! A celebration it is! Let me think about what kind of trip I can plan and we'll have one spectacular, romantic reconciliation celebration! I'll do all the planning, it's the least I can do after all the hurt that I caused you," he said.

"Babe, I can think of some other things that you can do to me to make up for what you did," I joked back with a little bit of a "bad girl" tone to my voice.

"That's my sweet girl. God, I've missed you. Missed the sound of your voice and that sexy little tone you get when you're bantering with me. Believe me, I will make it all up to you in ways that you can't even imagine. Get ready for the time of your life, babe! I'm going to make you happier than you could ever imagine possible," he lovingly said to me.

And after all that's happened, I believed him.

I had to.

"I can hardly wait. This calls for some major lingerie shopping, don't you think? Any requests?" I teased him.

"Nothing fancy required other than your beautiful naked body. It's all I want and all I need. Just looking at you like that gets me excited! No sexy undergarments required!" he teased back.

"Okay, then. Our one year anniversary is about a month away. Does that give you enough time for a trip and can you wait that long for me?" I asked.

"More than enough time, and no, I can't and won't wait that long. When can you get up here to the office? I have an idea. Tell Richie that you're going out with Colleen for the night. Then get that sexy little body of yours up here as fast as you can. Sound like a plan?" he asked, the excitement in his voice rising to what I imagined equaled the "rising" excitement somewhere else!

"I'll tell him on Monday that I'm going to meet Colleen for dinner on the turnpike. I'll see your cute little butt around six," I said.

"It's a plan. I love you for so many reasons, babe, but most of all for doing this," he said.

"I love you, too but I gotta go now and feed these children," I said, realizing that it was almost dinner time and I hadn't even started cooking yet.

"Okay I'll let you get off the phone but I'll never let you go out of my life again, ever. I love you," John said.

"I love you, too. Bye," I said as I hung up the phone.

I headed downstairs to start dinner, finding myself getting caught up in the kids gossip about how their day at school was and helping with homework assignments.

It's amazing how a woman can be so many different people - from being a mom, to a wife, to a lover.

All roles take on a life of their own transforming you in ways that you never could have imagined.

And I was living in all three of them.

John and I had managed to keep our relationship going for a few months, racking up phone bills that drove our parents over the edge, seeing each other only at Thanksgiving and Christmas. We'd blown most of our money on those trips back in September and our parents weren't giving us as much cash because of the phone bills.

We seemed to be "stuck" with the hurt that came from missing one another. John was drinking more and more and I was beginning to think of finding comfort in another way - in someone else's arms.

I met Steve innocently enough. It was a glance across the cafeteria at school. Once our eyes met he began to show up more and more wherever I was. Before long I found myself thinking less of John and more of Steve. I have to say, it sure was making the hurt bearable and the missing less.

I knew this wasn't the right thing to do but the times that John and I spoke by phone were becoming less and less. We'd go days without speaking to one another. Most times that I would call his roommate would be on the other end of the phone telling me that John was out. My mind could only imagine what he was doing on those nights out without me, especially since we barely spoke anymore

One night Steve kissed me and I realized that he was either my answer to hurting over John or my question about how I could be thinking of someone besides John.

If I couldn't be with John, this was the next best thing. And I liked Steve. He made me laugh and that's something that I hadn't done in a long time.

And he seemed to really like me.

We began hanging out together more and more and spending all of our weekends together. Then one night following a college party at Silver Lake we wound up back in his dorm room.

And we made love.

Or maybe we just had sex.

Maybe it was a little bit of both.

I knew that it was over with John and I had to tell him. I had been dodging his calls all week and knew now that I had to call and tell him the one thing that he had been so afraid of.

I had to tell him that I was leaving him.

I called John on a Thursday night and spit the whole story out in one fell swoop.

"You know that it's been rough with us, John. We're both miserable without each other and it shouldn't have to be that way. You barely call me anymore and when you do it's as if you're high or drunk. You don't even tell me how much you love me anymore. It's as if everything got ruined when we went to school," I said.

There was silence on the other end of the phone.

"John? Are you still there?" I asked.

"Yeah," he answered.

"I think that we should see other people, you know, so that we won't be missing each other as much," I said.

Again, dead silence on the other end of the phone.

"John, are you there?" I asked yet again.

"I'm here but I guess you're not. Who is he?" he asked, as if he already knew that I had met someone. I thought long and hard about what I was going to say, what I would say, what I should say.

"Answer me, dammit! I deserve the fucking truth!" he yelled. I could tell by his voice that he had been drinking, and drinking a lot, and stoned on top of that, I was sure.

"Okay, I did meet someone but it's not that I was looking for anyone. It just happened, you know?" I said sheepishly.

"What happened?" he asked. "What happened, did you sleep with him?"

I took a deep breath before I answered "Yes."

"How could you do that to me? I love you, did you forget that? We have plans for a future together or did you forget that?" he yelled.

"I love you, too, but I can't stand feeling this awful over missing you. It hurts too much and I can't concentrate on my school work. I don't sleep or eat and I'm sick all the time. I just can't do this anymore. If we're meant to be then it will be but I need a break. I'm so sorry," I said.

And I was sorry about hurting him. I did still love him but I was beginning to have feelings for Steve and they felt good.

"I guess that's it then, huh? We're over. Have fun with your new boyfriend and enjoy yourself since now you don't have to miss me," he said with an anger almost foreign to me.

"John, please don't be that way. I really am sorry. Don't hate me, please don't hate me," I said, feeling the tears welling up in my eyes.

"How could I hate you? I love you and I will for the rest of my life. I'm just hurt and mad and I need to get off the phone right now, okay?" he asked. I could tell that he was crying.

"Okay, I get it, but do me a favor, please cut back on your drinking and smoking, okay? I'm afraid that it's starting to become a problem," I said to him with concern.

"I'm not your worry anymore and my drinking and smoking is none of your fucking business," he barked back at me. "I have to go. Bye," he said and with that he hung up the phone.

Actually, judging by the sound I'd say that he "slammed" the phone down.

I hung up the receiver and walked slowly back to my room where Steve was waiting for me. He was sitting on my bed and looking straight into my eyes, the tears rolling down my cheek.

"Don't cry. It'll be alright. I'm here for you and he'll be okay. It's just a hit to a guy's ego when a girl dumps him. Don't worry about it, and don't worry about him," Steve said, pulling me down to sit down next to him on the bed. He put his arm around me and I cried into his shoulder, just as I had many times with John.

But this wasn't John.

"He'll be fine. Guys get over that kind of stuff," Steve said.

But I knew John and after hearing his voice over the phone I knew that he'd never get over this.

Not ever.

Chapter 37

The weekend was over and once again it was Monday. I had already spoken to Richie about "meeting Colleen" for dinner and it was just fine by him. In fact, he was planning on leaving work early to be home with the kids.

I went through the usual routine of female pampering before I was to meet John. I decided to wear a camel colored suede skirt and a black shirt with my black boots. In fact, I was definitely in the "bad girl" frame of mine so I added a black, silk thong to the "ensemble." There would be no pantyhose on this outing! I certainly had a plan for tonight and "easy on, easy off" was a part of it.

I fed the kids dinner and was out the door, passing Richie on his way into the house.

"I gotta run or I'll be late, see 'ya later," I said to him. "I left you a plate of dinner in the microwave. Just heat it up."

"Thanks! Have a good time and be careful driving home. Hey, wasn't it cool that Johnny let me leave early today? He's a great guy," he said.

Jesus, Richie, if you only knew!

And if you only knew what that "great guy" was about to do to your wife!

I was nervous driving up to see John. It was that kind of nervousness that you feel on a first date. It'd been awhile, a few months actually, since Miami and we were just getting back together.

195

That's the thing I've learned about having an affair. There's good and bad about it. The good thing is that everytime feels like the first time. The bad thing is that everytime feels like the first time with all the nervousness that comes with it. I wondered if there would ever come a time when I wasn't feeling nervous to be with John, nervous about his expectations or how my body looked to him.

Maybe the nervousness can be good because with it comes the excitement of the feelings of the "first time," yet it's nerve wracking, always wondering if you measure up, if you're good enough, if you're better than his wife.

I knew how John felt about me but that didn't mean that's how I felt about me.

It's too late now.

I jumped and was about to jump right onto him.

The drive took longer than I had expected. I had forgotten about that damn five o'clock rush hour traffic. Still, I ended up pulling into the parking lot around six thirty. I called John on his cell phone to make sure that the coast was clear. He assured me that it was.

I parked and practically ran out of the car and across the parking lot. It seemed as though the elevator took forever to transport me up to John's floor. Next thing I knew I heard the ding of the door as it opened and I ran down the hallway towards John's office. He was waiting for me in front of his door.

I ran straight into his arms, jumped up on him and wrapped my legs around his waist. He held me tight in his arms as our lips locked together and he carried me that way into his office, kicking the door shut with his foot.

John moved towards his desk and plopped me down on top of it. He cupped my face with his hands and showered me with kisses. I closed my eyes as if to savor every moment. His hands reached up under my skirt, sliding slowly along my thighs. He let out a dirty little laugh when he realized that I was wearing a thong.

I could feel the hardness of him pressing into me. He slid the thong down my legs, grabbed them up into his hands and pressed them to his face. He closed his eyes and inhaled my scent, the essence of my being.

Then he tossed them onto the couch.

I unbuckled his belt, unzipped his pants and slid them down to his ankles. He kicked them off and turned me around to face the desk, his front pressing hard into my back. His hands were still up my skirt, enticing me to the peak of excitement, to that point of no return.

He raised my skirt up to my hips and entered me from behind. We both let out a groan of ecstasy as being one, at being linked together again. He began the rhythm that he knew I liked and I reciprocated by rolling my hips around and around. It sounded as though he was laughing but he was having the time of his life and so was I.

He continued making love to me from behind until he pulled out, spun me around and sat me up on the top of the desk, pushing everything on it out of the way and onto the floor. I heard something break as it fell and when I glanced down to the floor I noticed that it was a picture of Tess and him. It was broken.

An omen, perhaps?

He kissed my face and neck, lifted my shirt over my head and took off my bra, tasting my nipples with his tongue, driving me completely wild.

"Make love to me...NOW!" I ordered him and with that he spread my legs wide open and entered me, thrusting harder and harder, deeper and deeper until we were ready to explode in passion together.

He looked into my eyes as he was still thrusting deep inside of me and whispered, "Come with me."

And I did.

And so did he.

We were both bathed in sweat by the time we were finished. John led me over to the couch. The leather felt cool on my hot, flushed skin and we snuggled deep into each other's arms. We stayed locked in this embrace until our heart beats slowed down to a normal pace.

He got up to get us each a bottle of water. As he took the top off to take a sip he licked all around the top of it and put it to my mouth. I closed my eyes as I took a sip, as if I were tasting him, and I was.

"Up for a trip back to Kennett?" he asked out of the blue.

"What? When?" I asked, still coming out of my stupor from our lovemaking.

"It's almost our one year anniversary, babe. I thought we should go away and celebrate," he said, taking another sip of water.

"Are you kidding? Oh my God, you are such a romantic! Back to the place where it all started. Give me the dates and you better believe that I'll be there," I said with all the excitement of a woman who just got a diamond from Tiffany's.

"I have it all planned out, babe, all you need to do is show up. I have something planned that will have that pretty little head of yours spinning," he said, making me wish that the trip was sooner than not.

"I just can't believe it! It's a dream come true! How long can you stay?" I asked.

"Three nights, sweet girl. Three whole nights with you and only you," he said.

I was filled with so much happiness right there and then that I didn't know what to do, yet within seconds I knew what to do.

I reached behind John to turn off the lights and knelt down on the floor in front of him. He smiled from ear to ear knowing what it was I was going to do.

"Want me to show you just how happy I am right now?" I teased.

"You better believe it. I'm ready for anything with you," he said as he rested his head back onto the couch, closed his eyes and took my head into my hands to guide me to where he wanted me to be.

And it's definitely where I wanted to be.

I took all of him into my mouth, sliding him deep inside and then out, using my tongue to lick every inch of him...

He groaned with pleasure and I was becoming wet from it.

This is where I wanted to be...

I wanted to be anywhere that John was.

I was working on Christmas Eve at a convenience store. There was no special person in my life at the time and no reason to be home. It was near eleven o'clock at night when the bells on the store door rang. I looked up from behind the register and there stood John.

"Oh my God! John! How in the hell did you find me?" I asked in utter surprise. My heart skipped a beat.

"Called your mom. She said that you were working until midnight. What the hell are you doing here on Christmas Eve?' he chided.

"I had nowhere and no one to be with so I figured what the hell...and it's overtime," I answered.

"Want to spend some time with me tonight?" he asked in a tone of voice that was quite familiar to me.

"Absolutely and I'm closing now anyway. Let me get my coat and I'll lock up. Follow me home and I'll change real quick. Then we can head out somewhere, if anywhere is open now," I said.

I put on my coat and locked the store door. John helped me into my car and told me to be careful driving home. It had started to snow and there was already a light coating on the street. He said that he'd follow me back to my house just in case anything should happen.

He followed me home and he chatted with my parents for a bit while I went upstairs to change and freshen up.

I hurried downstairs, we said goodbye to my parents and we got into his car to head to his house. He told me that his mother would be out until very late and the house was ours! I knew exactly what that meant and I was all for it. I had really missed him!

The snow was coming down a bit heavier now and we seemed to be the only people on the road. We got to his house and he walked me right to his bedroom. His room looked so different because so much of his things were still at school.

But it still had his scent to it.

Weed and cologne.

He pulled out a joint and lit it, offering me a hit. What the hell, I thought, this night is already fucked up, I might as well be too!

I took a hit and we passed it back and forth. I could already feel my body start to relax and melt. My head was dizzy but in a good way. I felt amazing.

John took the last hit but turned to me, took my chin in his hand and lifted my face towards his. He put his lips close to mine and blew the smoke into it. I held it deep inside before I exhaled.

He was looking deep into my eyes yet we didn't speak.

He waited for a split second, although when you're stoned it seems longer, and started to take my clothes off. He lifted my shirt above my head and unhooked the clasps of my bra. He placed them gently onto the chair at his desk. He unzipped my pants and started to pull them over my hips and down my thighs. When they reached my ankles he took them off. My thong was still on so he moved back up slowly to grab onto them with his teeth and pull them down my legs until he threw them off.

My head was dizzy from the pot and from John.

I started to undress him next, pulling his sweater up and over his head, then unbuckling his belt so that I could unzip his pants and pull them off. I used both hands to pull his boxers off and remove the last piece of clothing that was standing between our bodies.

And now they were two naked bodies.

He pulled me close and threw me down onto the bed. We made love to each other with a passion that I hadn't felt since the last time I was with him. It was a passion that I hadn't felt with anyone else, not even Steve.

We didn't speak much because there wasn't much to say. We could read each other's minds, we always could.

The only words that we spoke to each other were the words that said it all: "I love you."

We held each other close in bed for about an hour then dressed. We knew that his mom would be home soon and that my parents would be waiting for me.

We put our coats on and headed out to the car, standing there gazing into each other's eyes as the snow fell softly down upon us.

"I love you so very much. You make my soul soar and my heart take flight," he said as he gently kissed the tip of my nose.

"You are my poet, John, and I love you, too. Always have, babe," I said, kissing him back.

"I have an idea. Let's elope tonight. Let's just say to hell with everyone and get married, right on Christmas. We'll wake up in the morning together and tell our families that this is the only Christmas present we wanted - a life together. Let's do it, John. We love each other so much, it's the right

thing to do," I said, knowing that if he said yes he'd make me the happiest girl in the world.

He stood there for what seemed an eternity and said, "I can't. It's not that I don't love you, God knows that I love you with all of my heart and soul, but I can't, not right now. Please understand."

I hardly knew what to say. I thought he would have jumped at the chance, especially after the night we just shared together.

We got into the car and he drove me home. I didn't understand anything that had happened or what was going on.

He kissed me goodbye, but this time the kiss felt different than all the other's ever had.

This kiss really was good-bye.

I walked into the house and watched him drive away.

I started to cry because I knew that I'd never see him again.

And I never did.

Until many years later.

Until fate brought us together at just the wrong time.

Chapter 38

The weeks flew by and I found myself back on the road again, heading to the place where it all began a year ago - Kennett Square. John and I were both on our way to meet for what would be our one year anniversary celebration. Together we had managed to sustain our relationship without suspicion from our spouses.

Our love for one another had grown deeper and our need to be together had grown stronger. This weekend would be filled with lovemaking and celebration, along with some quiet time for us to have "the discussion." We had agreed that we would make the time on this trip to discuss our future together and where our relationship would go from here.

My mind was filled with thoughts about what our decision would be, of what HIS decision would be.

Would we keep things moving along as they were, stealing moments of passion wherever and whenever we could find them, or would we decide to end the relationship, the affair, with each of us going home to empty marriages?

I knew what I wanted to do but as always, I took my cues from John. I didn't want to be demanding, asking for the things which I knew he couldn't give me. I just wanted to love him and be with him, on his terms, no matter how much they hurt me or compromised my wants and needs. He had become my entire world, maybe he always was. Maybe our finding each other again woke me up to all that I was missing in my life.

I was missing being loved.

I thought about how my children would feel if I decided to leave their father. They would be hurt, that was certain, and it would break my heart, but their mother was a broken woman, merely a shell going through the daily motions of life, only coming to life when she was with John. I was certain that in time my children would understand this and accept it.

Maybe seeing their mother whole, healed and happy would be enough for them to understand my decision.

Yet with your children you just never know.

I saw the signs for my exit and proceeded to turn off. My palms were starting to sweat at the realization that only several miles down the road was the hotel, the one where he and I had first made love, the place where it all began just one year ago.

A few more minutes of driving found me turning into the hotel parking lot. I parked the car, opened the door and grabbed my suitcase. As I walked towards the lobby I saw John sitting on a bench, a bouquet of red roses in his hand. He was smiling from ear to ear, his face all aglow at seeing me. It looked as though he had a tear in his eyes, a tear of sheer joy and happiness.

I loved his smile. It could always melt away my fears and worries in an instant. I rushed to him, dropped my suitcase and fell into his arms which he wrapped tightly around me, the bouquet of roses in his hand now pressed into my lower back.

"Happy Anniversary, babe," he said, sealing his sentiment with a long passionate kiss.

"Right back at 'ya, love," I whispered into his ear.

He took my suitcase from me, I took the flowers from him and we proceeded to head up to our room, hand in hand. We got into the elevator staring into each other's eyes for the ride up to our floor, both of us smiling at one another with an excitement that you see on the faces of children on Christmas morning.

The elevator stopped at the third floor and we stepped out. He led me down the hall to room 323.

"I can't believe you remembered," I said to him with great surprise.

"Sure I remembered! How could I have forgotten one of the most important moments of my life? I remember everything, babe, EVERYTHING! And I only got one room. There will be no more of me walking down the hall to my room, this is all ours," he said, his lips brushing the top of my head.

He put the key card into the door and pushed it open, holding it open as I walked in. I couldn't believe what I saw before me.

The curtains were drawn, giving the room the appearance of a late evening, even though it was only six o'clock. Candles were lit and placed strategically around the room, casting a beautiful, soft glow upon our bed. As I stepped in further I noticed a trail of red rose petals strewn around the room, encircling the bed. The blankets had been turned down, rose petals placed all over the sheets and pillows. A bottle of my favorite wine was chilling on the nightstand in a shiny, silver bucket along with a plate of some very seductive looking chocolate covered strawberries, another one of my favorites.

"Oh, John, I don't know what to say! I can't believe that you did all of this for me. It's beautiful. It's perfect! What could I possibly do for you that could even compare or come close?" I asked.

He pulled me close into him, wrapped his arms around me and kissed me hard.

"Oh, babe, I could think of a few things. Did you say come close?" he said with a devilish school boy tone to his voice, a huge grin on his face. He started to chuckle in a flirty kind of way.

"Well, then," I said, pushing him closer and closer to the bed, "I'm your girl!" "You always have been," he said.

I slipped his polo shirt up over his head, kissing his chest, his shoulders, his neck, and then I moved my hands lower to unbuckle his belt, unbuttoning the top of his khaki pants then unzippering them. I slid them slowly down past his hips, past his knees until they dropped to the floor. He stepped out of them as he began to take off his boxers but I grabbed his hands and said, "No, I got this."

He closed his eyes and let me finish the task that I had started.

Without speaking he pulled my black tank top up and over my head, my nipples already hard with excitement, my body getting hotter and hotter with each touch of his hands on my bare skin. His hands moved downward to undo my jeans, sliding them down to my ankles. He began to kiss my neck, intermittently licking my skin as he moved his body downward along mine.

His tongue played with my nipples and his hands with my breasts, arousing them even more. Then he began moving ever so slowly down to my waist where he grabbed my thong with his teeth, just as he had done so many times before, pulling them off with his mouth, down to my ankles where I stepped out of them. He took a sniff of my essence on them and threw them to the floor.

He moved down in front of me and got on his knees, where he stayed as he caressed my naked body with his hands, tasting my essence with his tongue. I closed my eyes, threw my head back and let my mind and body drift to the place where only he could take me

After a few moments passed he slowly stood up, his lips glistening with "me" on them, and gently moved me onto the bed. As I lay there he stood over me, staring at my naked and wet body from head to toe.

"My heart's taking a picture," he whispered.

He took several of the roses from my bouquet and began pulling off the petals, sprinkling them all over my body. He slid down on top of me, his hands moving in slow motion all over my body, his touch igniting a fire deep inside of me. It was at that moment I opened myself to take all of him inside of me and it was then that our love for each other flowed between us. I could feel him inside of me, touching places that only he could inspire to feel this way.

Our passion grew with every moment, with every rise and flow of our lovemaking, until at last our love exploded in sync with each other. My love for him now spilled wildly all over him, his love for me filling me deep inside.

He rolled to the side and took me into his arms, kissing my forehead which was now glistening with sweat. I lay my head onto his chest, inhaling the scent of how his body smells after making love to me, a scent I had grown accustomed to. Our feet were tangled together, our bodies which were hot with passion just moments ago now cooling down from the sweat which covered our naked bodies.

John pulled the blanket up over us, turned to his side and propped himself up with his arm, looking me right in the eyes.

"I'm leaving Tess," he said matter of factly.

"What?" I said, my mind quickly coming out of the hazy fog it had been in for the last hour or so.

"I'm leaving her. I want you and only you and I'm sick and tired of all this sneaking around. We should have been together from the start and it's about time that we both faced up to that. I want to spend the rest of my life with you. What do you think of that?" he asked calmly, yet with anticipation at what my response would be.

I couldn't believe what I was hearing. I'm sure that I had shaken my head a few times as if trying to clear my ears, hoping that I heard him correctly.

"Oh my God, John, are you sure? Are you really sure because I can't take another heartbreak," I answered.

"More sure than I've ever been about anything in my life. I decided that this is what I wanted a few weeks ago but I wanted to wait until our special weekend to tell you. Makes it all that much more romantic, don't you think?" he said ever so lovingly.

"Romantic? Absolutely and you know what? I'm sure too, sure that I'm ready to leave Richie and be with you. I've been ready to leave him for a long time, I've just been waiting for you. I've been waiting for you for over 25 years," I said, kissing him on the mouth.

I kept kissing him, over and over again, until both of us started laughing and giggling with excitement and happiness over the decision we were making. Our relationship would now be out in the open for everyone to know and for everyone to see.

John poured us each a glass of wine and we fed each other strawberries, chatting endlessly about how wonderful our lives were going to be now, of how we would blend our families, of how our children would love each other and of how life was going to be absolutely perfect.

And at this very moment life was perfect.

We made love again, but it felt different this time. It felt better. This time we knew that we were making love to each other and our future together. We'd never have to hide this magical, wonderful love again.

When we were done John told me to reach under my pillow. I slid my hand under it and pulled out a small box wrapped in red satin ribbon. I opened it slowly, my hands shaking with excitement over the thought of what was probably in it.

I slowly untied the ribbon and opened the box. My heart at the sight I saw before my eyes. It was a beautiful white gold ring set with a heart shaped diamond.

"Marry me," he said, grinning from ear to ear. "Marry me and make all my dreams come true."

"John, yes, I'll marry you and you must know, my love, that at this very moment you just made all of my dreams come true," I answered, tears of sheer happiness falling from my eyes.

He took the ring from the box and placed it on my left hand onto the finger which used to have my wedding ring on it. I had taken that off a year ago.

He put his arms around me and lay his head on my shoulder and I could feel the tears flowing from his eyes wetting my shirt. It was a moment I'd never forget. A moment that my heart took a picture. A moment that my heart memorized.

"Let's take a drive," he said. "It's a beautiful night out and I want to keep this celebration going!"

"Sounds like a plan. I'm in!" I said excitedly.

We hopped out of bed and dressed, kissing each other as we put on each piece of clothing. I was glad to go for a drive with him. It's something we always loved to do together as far back as high school. We'd put on our favorite music, hold hands and kiss at the red lights. I couldn't wait to go on a drive with my soon to be husband.

"Just think, babe, this is a new beginning for us. A brand new start to a brand new life together. Let's hit the road, it'll be the first ride of many to come as Mr. and Mrs.!" he said with a sound to his voice that I hadn't ever heard before, one of ultimate happiness in knowing that we'd finally made our decision about "us."

And this time it was the right decision.

As we walked out of the hotel and into the parking lot there she was, "Rosie." It was a replica of "our car" from our high school days. It's the one we first made love in at the mall. This night was all too perfect. Suddenly we were back to being 17, no cares or worries and once again having a lifetime ahead of us.

I had a tear in my eye seeing "her," our "Rosie."

John opened the car door for me and made sure that I was all buckled in. He was such a stickler for safety, much different than he had been back in high school. He slid into his seat, buckled in and we were off.

The night was warm and balmy, the skies clear and filled with a million stars. The almost full moon was shining brightly, illuminating the world around us as if it were daytime. This would be the perfect night for a long drive with the man I love, the man of my dreams. I couldn't help but think of one of our high school drives so many years ago.

"Come on! Hurry up! I've got an ice cold six pack in the car and I don't want it to get warm, hurry up, babe!" John yelled to me as I was running out of my house. It was the summer of 1979, the summer after our high school graduation.

I slid into his 1972 Chevy Chevelle, "Rosie," as we named her, and across the beach seat. He put his arm around me and we were off.

"Where are we going tonight?" I asked, popping open a beer to share with him.

"For a drive to the beach," he said as he sped out of my parents driveway. John loved to drive, it seems like most of our dates were "road trips," but I loved driving with him. It was as though driving transported him to a different world, one without worries or cares. He was so happy driving around with me, our bodies touching together.

I took a sip of beer and held it up to his mouth to offer him one. We drove for miles along the beach, smoking cigarettes and drinking beer until we found "our beach."

He pulled the car into the parking space, grabbed the remaining beers and a blanket and we walked together onto the beach. There weren't many people down here tonight. It seemed as though we were the only two there.

A lifeguard stand had been left up so we climbed up onto it and nestled into each other's arms, staring out at the ocean and looking up at the stars. We drank more beers and talked and talked.

We talked about our hopes for college and about our future together. Our mouths met one another and we kissed for hours.

John began singing to me and my heart melted even more.

I love this guy so much, I thought, I can't wait until college is over so that we can get married.

This was true happiness, a love so pure and untarnished.

This was exactly what I had hoped my life to be like.

I wanted to stay in this moment forever.

But forever doesn't always last even though I had hoped it would.

Chapter 39

John held my hand tightly in his as we drove, singing along with the song on the radio. He'd look over at me now and again, smiling and telling me how happy that I had made him.

Funny, I thought to myself, I was just thinking about how happy he made me.

We drove for what seemed like an hour when we decided to head back to the hotel. The passion between us was building and both of us wanted to be back in bed together, sharing ourselves with each other and sharing our love for one another…together.

John pulled into a Dunkin' Donuts parking lot to turn around.

"Let's get a cup of coffee. I want us to be up all night tonight," he said with a twinkle in his eye.

"I don't need coffee for that, love," I joked with him, "but if you want coffee, we'll get coffee."

I ran into the store, ordered two coffees, paid for them and got back into the car. He pulled out of the parking lot and we were on our way back to the hotel.

We had only been on the road a few moments before we realized that we were going in the wrong direction, finding ourselves in a wooded part of town, not the busy city that we had just driven through.

"Shit, we're lost. Let me turn around again," John said, with just a touch of annoyance in his voice and a slight sound of fear in not knowing where we were.

"It's okay, babe. We're together and who knows, maybe we'll see something interesting. You and I could never be lost. We're found, love," I said back to him hoping to break his slightly agitated mood.

"Jesus, do you always see the bright side?" he chided me back.

"Yes, and I'm looking directly at my bright side!" I said back to him, smiling. "Babe, what would I do without you? You are my anchor, the girl that keeps me grounded in times like these," he said as he took my hand and kissed the top of it. It was his way of telling me that he loved me.

Yet again, he had a million ways of telling me and showing me that he loved me.

"You'll never have to wonder, my love," I said.

We hadn't been driving for more than a few minutes when we saw something ahead in the road. At first we thought it was a deer and that it would move as we got closer.

But it didn't move and before we knew it we could see that it was a large box or something that a truck must have dropped in the road. John wasn't driving very fast but he had to think fast and that meant that we'd have to swerve to avoid it and we were surrounded by trees.

Within seconds it happened, within seconds everything happened.

The last thing I remember was John yelling something to me and his arm being forcefully thrown against my chest to protect me from the impact, the kind of move a parent makes on their child when they stop short.

I don't remember much after that or how much time had passed but I found myself waking up as if I were waking up from a deep sleep. I was groggy and my body hurt all over.

John's arm, which had once been forcefully placed against my chest, was now lying limp on my lap. I turned my head to look over at him.

His head was lying limp on the steering wheel, covered in blood. I'd never seen so much blood. It was everywhere.

I grabbed his hand that was in my lap and felt nothing. No squeeze back as he had done so often, no warmth of his skin, no pulse. I looked down at my left hand at the ring that John had just given me, now splattered in blood, in his blood, illuminated by the light of the moon.

I looked back at him and in that split second my heart broke and I knew he was gone.

And that's the last thing I remember before I lost consciousness.

"We should get home. I do believe that the sun will be coming up soon and your parents will be less than thrilled that I kept their daughter out all night," John said.

"You worry too much! I'll handle them. Just a few more minutes, please?" I begged him in a very flirtatious way.

"You know that I can't say no to you. Just another five, sweet girl," John said, starting to kiss me again.

We packed up and left the beach. He took the long way home, knowing how much I hated to say goodbye to him. Before long we were at my house and were exchanging our last kisses for the night.

"I love you, John," I said.

"I love you, too. I'll see you in the morning," he said as he opened the car door for me to walk me to my front door.

"Call me when you get home. You know that I can't sleep until I know you're safe..." I said as I hugged him goodnight.

Chapter 40

I woke up three days later, Richie sitting in a chair in the corner of my hospital room. His face was blank, a solemn look upon it.

"You were in a bad car accident with John. He didn't make it. Tess and I have talked and we know everything that went on between the two of you for the last year. At least you made it out of the accident with your life," he said in a stoic voice.

I could barely wrap my head around what he was saying. John? Dead?

"John is dead? Are you sure?" I asked in a soft whisper, tears beginning to well up in my eyes. I was beginning to remember the accident but was so hoping that I remembered it wrong.

"Yes, he died. Let it go. He's gone and you're not. We'll get through this. We'll work things out. I can get over what you did, of all the things you did, and soon everything will get back to normal. It'll be just like nothing ever happened," Richie said, his voice in one steady tone.

I turned my head and looked out of the window, pain filling every inch of my body and I began to sob uncontrollably. The tears stung the cuts on my face and I couldn't tell what hurt more, my body or my heart.

Oh, God, he's gone, he's gone, I thought to myself, but then again, I think I may have screamed it out loud. I remember hearing Richie call for the nurse to come in and give me more pain medication.

Together forever, babe. You and me. I'm more sure about you and I than anything else in my life. Marry me and make my dreams come true," echoed through my mind day and night.

Chapter 41

It's been a month since the accident. I was released from the hospital after about a week with lacerations to my face, a broken arm and a sprained ankle. The doctor had given me some wonderfully strong pain medication, which I took religiously every four hours. The pain had subsided in my body but the pain in my heart grew more and more unbearable with each day that passed.

Richie stayed home with me for the first week after I was released from the hospital. He was nice and polite but the mood in my house was somber, as if a dark cloud had planted itself over it. My children were relieved to know that I hadn't died like "daddy's boss" but were scared to death at how broken up I looked. Thank God that they couldn't see how broken up I was inside.

They didn't know about John and I but they knew that something wasn't quite right with me. They could sense it and could see it. I didn't smile, I didn't laugh. I was there in body but my spirit had taken flight with John's the night he died.

Oh my God, "he died."

I couldn't wrap my head around the fact that my John died.

My mother came to stay with me and the kids after Richie went back to work. She didn't want me home alone with the kids and felt as though she had to do something to keep her mind off of what her daughter had done. I'm sure I was a disappointment to her but was thankful she was here to take care of me and my children because Lord knows that right now I couldn't take care of them. I couldn't even take care of myself.

Richie endured his own private hell at the office, co-workers whispering over the water cooler and flowers of condolences placed outside of John's office door. They were polite enough, no one asking questions, just offering him sympathy. I'm guessing that it was sympathy towards his wife breaking his heart, not of his wife being injured.

Tess had cleaned John's office out of his personal things, finding copies of all our emails, having access to his cell and all of our text messages, the cards and pictures of John and me. She had had coffee with Richie once that I knew of, both of them offering each other their sympathy and understanding. Richie offered his apology for a wife that couldn't be faithful to her husband and keep her hands off of hers.

She didn't offer anything back to him except a dirty look, a cold shoulder and a "fuck your wife."

She did, however, give him all of the pictures of John and I and told him to do with them what he wanted. She wanted no memory of that time and although she was hurt over the loss of her husband, she hated him and me.

Who could blame her?

My mother, who was normally critical over my every move, was unusually polite and kind, making me uncomfortable. But she knew the story. Everyone knew the story now, but no one knew what to do or say and I could have cared less.

Life went on as it normally did even after all of this, waking every morning to the sounds of the kids bickering as they got ready for school and me trying to get them out the door for the bus. I couldn't wait for them to leave. I couldn't stand being around them because when I was I couldn't show them the pain I was in both physically and emotionally. I had to be strong, yet I was unable to.

My heart was broken beyond repair and day by day I could feel myself slipping away into a place that I had never been to before. I was scared because I really didn't know how to live without John. Every moment of every day I had to remind myself to "breathe."

Sleeping pills that the hospital had given me were the only thing I looked forward to because in my sleep John was there. He consumed my every sleeping moment. It was in my dreams that we talked, laughed and made love. In my dreams I could feel him, see him, smell him.

In my dreams I could be with him.

"I need to run to the store. Will you be okay for an hour or two?" my mom asked.

"Sure, I'll be fine. Go," I answered with a hint of relief in knowing that I'd finally be alone. The kids wouldn't be home from school for a few hours.

"Need anything while I'm out? Anything special?" she asked.

"NO! I don't fucking need anything or anyone. The one thing that I want I can't have, not now, not ever, okay?" I barked at her.

"Okay," she answered quietly. I would have apologized to her, because I owed her that, but I wasn't in the mood.

I heard the car pull out of the driveway. I was alone, thank God.

I made a cup of coffee and stood in the kitchen. I don't know how long I was standing there but it must have been for quite awhile because when I finally took a sip of my coffee it was cold.

Suddenly thoughts of John flooded my mind and I found myself letting out a cry that came from somewhere deep down inside of me.

I collapsed onto the floor, the coffee mug hitting the floor, shattering and spilling coffee everywhere. I sat there all curled up, letting out tears that had been locked up since the accident. My mind was filled with thoughts of John and what we had lost, what was stolen from us.

My heart no longer functioned, it was broken beyond repair and I knew that I would never find myself again, never be who I was again. The tears were streaming so violently down my face that I could barely see.

I think I had been screaming because my screaming turned to shrieks and I felt as though in one split second my mind exploded…

And I believe that it did.

I barely remember getting up off the floor but I must have because I found myself back up in my bedroom, my bottle of sleeping pills and pain pills in hand.

I took one, then two, then three, and then I stopped counting.

I turned on the radio, John's and my favorite station, and laid down on the bed. The music was playing softly and the pills were starting to do something wonderful or maybe awful to me.

My stomach was starting to hurt and my body felt strange. My mind was fuzzy but I tried to focus.

I had to find John.

Where is he?

The empty pill bottles lay beside me and everything else became just a blur in front of me.

Then, suddenly, there he was.

John was here.

He was standing next to me, his hand outstretched towards me like it had been so many times.

"What's wrong, my sweet girl? Don't cry, please don't cry. I'm here," he said as his hand wipes the tears that fell softly down my cheeks.

"John," I said out loud. I couldn't see anything in the room except John. I reached my hand out to grab onto his and for the first time since the accident I could feel him, felt his fingers entwined with mine.

He grabbed my hand tightly and smiled, that ear to ear grin that I fell in love with so many years ago.

"Come with me and we'll make all of our dreams come true," he said, coaxing me out of the bed.

"You are the love of my life and all of my dreams have come true now," was the last thing I said. My body felt a peace that I hadn't felt since John died.

I felt his warmth, his love, his being and I knew that I'd go anywhere with him...

To the ends of the earth...

And now I was on a path to heaven with him...

Or maybe it was hell.

As I rose from the bed, hand in hand with John, our favorite song was playing on the radio.

It's the last thing I remembered echoing through my mind before...

"I love you, my sweet girl. Let's make our dreams come true..."

220 221 222

Cover design by: Bill Scannell

As a lifelong resident of the Jersey Shore, photography has always been a part of my life. After recovering from the effects of cancer treatments, photography actually became a healing avenue for me. It got me out and enjoying life again. My skills in photo editing helps me craft visually appealing pieces of art and that's just the beginning of what has led me to designing this book cover. Photography brings a deeper connection with whatever it is you are trying to capture.

Instagram: billscannell

About the Author

Anne Dennish is the author of "Waking Up: Lessons Learned Through My Adventures With Life and Breast Cancer," "My Collective Soul: Things I Know Without Knowing Why" and "Each Breath Along The Journey." She lives on the West Coast of Florida doing what she can to make this world a better place.

Annedennish.com
Instagram: anne_dennish
Facebook: Anne Dennish

For more information, contact Anne at annedennish@gmail.com
The story of "The Mind of a Heart" continues
in late 2024 with "One Last Look"

Printed in the United States
by Baker & Taylor Publisher Services